"I kn... ,
Annie murmured.

She touched his cheek. She felt him relax, and he finally looked at her.

"Think so?" Amusement hovered in his lazy syllables. "I doubt it. Annie, you don't strike me as someone who's carrying a world-class load of experience around on your shoulders." Slowly, regretfully, he tiptoed his fingers down the vertebrae of her spine, one by one, until he clasped her hips and lifted her off his lap.

"It was only a kiss." She smoothed her skirt down.

"Since the moment you walked into the Star, I've wondered what it would be like to kiss you, Angel-Annie, *really* kiss you. Believe me," he said, looking up at her, "this was something outside my experience."

Standing over him, Annie reached out her hand. "Whatever it was, I don't regret it."

"I do," he muttered. "And you should."

Dear Reader,

A gift from the heart, from us to you—this month's special collection of love stories, filled with the spirit of the holiday season. And what better place to find romance this time of year than UNDER THE MISTLETOE?

In *Daddy's Angel,* favorite author Annette Broadrick spins a tale full of charm and magic—and featuring FABULOUS FATHER Bret Bishop. Treetop angel Noelle St. Nichols visits this single dad and the children she's cherished from afar—and suddenly longs to trade her wings for love.

Annie and the Wise Men by Lindsay Longford is the heartwarming story of Annie Conroy and her kids, as their search for a temporary home on the holiday lands them face-to-face with a handsome young "Scrooge," Ben Jackson.

And Carla Cassidy will persuade you to believe once again that Santa Claus is not only alive and well—he's in love! Someone up above must have known that rugged Chris Kringle was just the man to make Julie Casswell smile again. Could it have been *The Littlest Matchmaker?*

More great books to look for this month include *A Precious Gift* by Jayne Addison, continuing the story of the lovable Falco family. Moyra Tarling shows us that *Christmas Wishes* really do come true in a moving story of a father reunited with his son by a spirited woman who believes in love. And there's love, laughter and merrymaking unlimited in Lauryn Chandler's *Romantics Anonymous*.

Wishing you a happy holiday and a wonderful New Year!

Anne Canadeo
Senior Editor

ANNIE AND
THE WISE MEN
Lindsay Longford

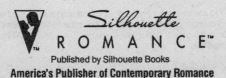

Silhouette
ROMANCE™
Published by Silhouette Books
America's Publisher of Contemporary Romance

To my friends in RWA:
Thank you for the lessons, the support, and the
kindness, and thanks, most of all, for the wonderful
books you've written—I'm jealous!

 SILHOUETTE BOOKS

ISBN 0-373-08977-5

ANNIE AND THE WISE MEN

Copyright © 1993 by Jimmie L. Morel

Books by Lindsay Longford

Silhouette Romance

Jake's Child #696
Pete's Dragon #854
Annie and the Wise Men #977

Silhouette Intimate Moments

Cade Boudreau's Revenge #390
Sullivan's Miracle #526

LINDSAY LONGFORD,

like most writers, is a reader. She even reads tooth-paste labels in desperation! A former high school English teacher with an M.A. in literature, she began writing romances because she wanted to create stories that touched readers' emotions by transporting them to a world where good things happened to good people and happily-ever-after is possible with a little work.

Her first book, *Jake's Child,* was nominated for Best New Series Author, Best Silhouette Romance and received a Special Achievement Award for Best First Series Book from *Romantic Times*. It was also a finalist for the Romance Writers of America RITA award for Best First Book.

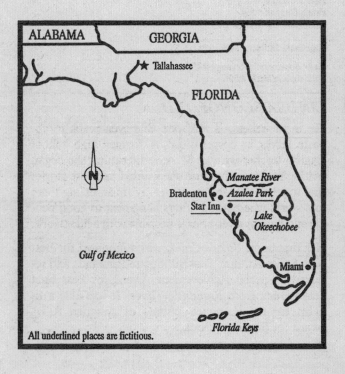

ALABAMA GEORGIA

★ Tallahassee

FLORIDA

Manatee River

Bradenton *Azalea Park*

Star Inn

Lake Okeechobee

Gulf of Mexico

Miami

Florida Keys

All underlined places are fictitious.

Chapter One

The bright red CHECK ENGINE light on the dashboard panel hypnotized Annie.

In the sudden silence as the car engine died, she gripped the steering wheel stiffly, wrapping her fingers around the hard plastic. *Go, go, go!* she whispered under her breath, hoping determination alone would bring back the comforting drone of the engine.

Broken only by the low beams of her headlights, the gray fog of the Florida night surrounded her as she guided the car to the side of the narrow road. Its momentum finally gone, the car coasted to a halt under a large oak tree garlanded with lacy shadows of moss and shining with fog-damp.

CHECK ENGINE. The panel light still glowed, Christmasy-red. Cheerful.

Annie stared at the message in the dim interior of the car. In her utter exhaustion, the words made as much sense to her as a message from outer space.

CHECK ENGINE.

Taking a deep breath, she looked away, unable to think about the meaning of those alarming words. Not now. Not when she was plummeting down a dark tunnel with no light in view. Please God, not one more disaster, she prayed.

Sometime during the last month of nights spent tossing and turning and not sleeping, she'd lost her ability to think clearly, her brain turning to jelly.

She felt like one of those roly-poly clown dolls. Hit 'em and they bounce back, again and again. But she didn't know how many more times she could take a licking and keep on ticking. Bouncing back took more and more energy lately.

Katie and Will. Her children. Despite the sick churning of her stomach, she concentrated on them and found, after all, a reservoir of energy. Katie and Will.

Ahead of her, beyond the comforting triangle of light cast by her headlights, the road disappeared into the misty night.

Behind her, December darkness, emptiness and Katie's huge, frightened eyes gazing back at her in the rearview mirror.

In the front seat beside Annie, unmoving, Will was a small, shadowy lump, legs dangling over the seat, hands clenched in his lap.

Nobody spoke.

From the shadows beyond the car, a bullfrog claimed his territory in a rhythmic bass *ba-rump, ba-rump, ba-rump*.

Not knowing what else to do, Annie turned off the ignition. The headlights winked off.

Wrapped in night shadows, she squinted through the bug-smeared windshield and strained for a glimpse of an oncoming vehicle, willed headlights to loom up out of the darkness.

For a brief second, she thought she saw a flicker of light through the trees ahead of her, but it was apparently only the product of wishful thinking. The glint of green she thought she saw glowed and vanished in the haze.

Annie knew what lay behind them. Fifty miles of rough concrete slashing through scrubland.

Her eyes burning with the effort to see *something, anything,* she blinked.

No cars had passed them in either direction for over an hour.

Her dreadful sense of direction had reared its malicious head, and in the darkness she'd missed the route markers for Sarasota. Twisting and backtracking, trying to correct her original error, she'd made wrong turn after wrong turn as the fog rolled in, stranding them God-only-knew-where.

She sure didn't.

And here they were—wherever *here* turned out to be—jobless, homeless, and stranded on some deserted Florida back road three days before Christmas.

Remembering how everything had gone wrong as fast as it could, Annie experienced again that quick scrabble of panic in her chest. Locked out of their Chicago apartment for nonpayment of rent, she'd seen Florida as their temporary refuge. Having talked to her grandmother only a few weeks earlier before their phone was disconnected, Annie had hoped to stay with her, to find a job and resettle the kids in school.

Old age and brittle bones had made that hope impossible.

Two weeks ago, Gramma Catherine had fallen and was in the nursing home where Annie had finally tracked her down.

Lying for all she was worth so as not to worry Gramma Catherine, Annie had sworn everything was now fine. Watching the lines of worry deepen in her grandmother's parchment-thin skin, Annie had embellished with every ounce of creativity in her. She'd found a job in Sarasota, she rattled on, and was going to be staying with a former high school friend, and all the while she'd smiled until her cheeks hurt while she tried to decide as fast as she could what in the world she was going to do next.

Leaving the nursing home, she'd believed things couldn't get worse.

They had.

She turned the ignition key. The motor cranked. Her pulse slowed as she gave a quick thumbs-up to Will.

Please, please...

The motor kept churning and churning, straining.

But it didn't catch and turn over.

Fighting the flutter of panic that made her fingertips tremble against the steering wheel, Annie turned off the engine again. The flutter spread to her stomach. She took deep breaths.

The sweet smell of orange blossoms flowed into the car through the open window. A warm breeze settled on her bare arms.

But she wanted the sharp bite of cold air, the sting of snow against her cheeks, not this sweet-scented Florida warmth seeping in on the foggy night.

She wanted a Christmas tree shining with small white lights and glittering with silver tinsel. She wanted to see shiny red bows marching haphazardly across its deep green branches. Planning and saving for the best Christmas ever, she and Katie and Will had spent an evening tying a wide spool of ribbon into fat bows.

Five days ago, the bows had been thrown any-which-way into a cardboard box and left for the garbage pickup.

Katie had seen an edge of ribbon and, white-faced and silent, carried the bows to the trunk of the car, tucking the box in with the suitcases and few belongings they'd salvaged.

Annie's eyes burned.

She'd dreamed of a Norman Rockwell Christmas.

What she'd gotten was a Freddy Kreuger nightmare.

The tiny pop as Katie stuck her thumb into her mouth almost made Annie bawl.

Instead, she half turned in her seat so that she could face Katie and Will. "Well, guys, looks like I took a wrong turn." In spite of her efforts, the last word wobbled.

Will, being Will, caught it. Seven years old going on forty, he offered comfort. "We been lost before. But only for a while. Until you figure it out, Mommy. And you do," he said earnestly, "usually."

"Of course I do. Sooner or later. Looks like this time it's going to be later, though." She made herself smile, inviting him to share the joke at her expense.

But his hands were still fisted in his lap, his solemn, thin face scrunched up with worry as he added in a low, shaky voice, "But the car never quit before." Scrupulously, he amended, "Maybe I didn't know?"

"No. I haven't had any trouble with the car until now. It's been dependable. We've been lucky." Annie listened for the whine of an engine outside, the hiss of tires against concrete.

Will's eyebrows met in the center of his forehead, but he didn't say a word as he watched her with his too-wise eyes.

"An old head on young shoulders," Gramma Catherine had said time and again about Will.

Annie wanted to haul him onto her lap and make the worry in his face go away. No matter how smart he was, he was still her baby.

She wanted to put her arms around her children, shut her eyes and wake up with their lives back to normal.

For a second, she actually shut her eyes. When she opened them, reality and the smell of oranges swamped her and she was still stranded alongside a deserted road.

Since she couldn't wave a magic wand, she smoothed down the stubborn lock of hair at the crown of her son's head. Her hand lingered for an instant at the nape of his neck, thin, wiry and vulnerable. "Hey, Will," she said softly, leaning close to him, "don't worry. That's my job. You're the kid. I'm the mom. Worrying is what I get paid for, okay?" She patted his narrow shoulder. "This is no big deal. Really. No problem. I can handle it."

As she kissed his cheek, Annie wondered who she was trying to convince. Will. Or herself.

"You can fix the car?" Tension still strung his body taut and there was no hope in his light blue eyes.

Even her children knew Annie didn't know beans about machinery and electrical appliances.

"Well, not exactly. Not the car, of course not. I can't fix the car." Thinking hard, Annie dug into the box of cookies between her and Will, handing one back to Katie.

Preferring her thumb for the moment, Katie shook her head.

Wiggling her finger under Katie's fist gripping the edge of the child seat, Annie sighed as Katie's hand closed around her mother's finger, small fist clutching firmly. Letting Katie cling to her, Annie glanced over her shoulder at Will. "But I'm pretty good at solving problems. Remember?"

The vertical crease in Will's forehead eased a bit. "Usually."

"Always," she insisted, shoving down her misgivings to give her son what reassurance she could. She knew the caution in his voice wasn't because of her, but Will and Katie had had too much upheaval in their short lives.

In the last eight years, she'd had enough uncertainty and changes to last her a lifetime, too. Stability and boredom had become very appealing. She stared into the blurry gray, the weight of her small family's welfare momentarily paralyzing her.

"Is it bad?" Anxiety pitched Will's voice high, and he sounded all of his seven years.

If one door slammed shut, there was always another one to bang open. Like the fog outside, the words hovered in the air, as real as if someone had spoken them aloud, and eased her raspy breathing.

"Listen, owl, we're not in the soup yet," she said, giving the first line of the game they played every time things looked desperate.

Katie squeezed Annie's finger. "P'tatah," she mumbled around her thumb.

"Oh, really? You'll be the potato in the soup? What about Will?"

Tilting her head, her plain little face suddenly transformed by her mischievous smile, Katie whispered, "Cawwot. Will k'n be a cawwot."

"No." Will frowned at Katie, his concern too great for distraction.

"Listen, guys, this is an adventure. That's what," Annie said as she surreptitiously turned the ignition key. "A challenge. Something to tell your kids about when you're old, okay?"

Katie and Will were silent.

The car labored mightily but nothing happened.

"Not the battery," Will said, pointing to the lights.

"No," Annie acknowledged as she switched off the engine.

"Control model, maybe," Will offered.

Listening carefully, Annie absently corrected him, "Module." Will plucked bits of information out of the air like dust specks. She'd learned it paid to heed his observations.

"In the distributor," he said, twisting his hands together.

"Distributor?" Annie echoed in the teeth of utter, absolute disaster.

"Skeeter said, maybe sometimes the distributor would make a car stop. Bang, bang, bump. Dead in the water," Will quoted. "Like ours did. The module in the distributor."

"Is this distributor thing expensive?" Giving the lie to her concern, Annie looked out casually at the trees and bushes.

Will nodded. "Two hundred dollars. Maybe."

Annie swallowed. Definitely expensive, especially right now.

Skeeter was the backyard mechanic who'd lived two houses down from their apartment. He'd taken care of her car for her, and Will had shadowed him, soaking up Skeeter's every word of wisdom. She'd frequently wished Will hadn't heard *everything* Skeeter said, but she'd adapted, figuring her son could do worse than listen to Skeeter, who was kind, honest and tolerant of his attentive little shadow.

And she was grateful, too, because Skeeter had saved her hundreds of dollars in car repairs as he kept her car running through three Chicago winters.

Unfortunately, there hadn't been time for Skeeter to give the car a last, quick checkup before they left.

"Skeeter said he was getting a car phone. *We* could use one," Will said, his voice tentative. "I wish we had one…" His voice trailed off into the night.

"Me, too." Annie stared at her son. She'd worked so hard to make their lives better, orderly, and now, no matter how hard she tried, everything was slipping through her fingers like water. "Oh, Will, I do, too." She squeezed his cold hands and turned back to the steering wheel.

Sending a tiny, heartfelt prayer once more to anybody who was listening, Annie tried the ignition one last time.

Clearly nobody was listening.

Not to her, anyway. She counted to ten and slowed her breathing.

Half a package of cookies wouldn't get her guys through the night. They'd drunk the last of the juice shortly after she'd made the first wrong turn. Although they'd already slept one night in the car, she'd planned supplies for that overnighter. Tonight, though, Will and Katie needed food, drink, a real bed and shower.

And on this road, there was no point waiting around for rescue.

Besides, what if no one rescued them tomorrow, either?

Thinking of that elusive wink of green in the mist, Annie made a decision.

She removed the key from the ignition, picked up her purse on the floor and tossed the useless piece of metal inside.

Finding courage, she injected enthusiasm into her voice. "Guys, this adventure is getting better. We're going exploring."

Quickly, leaving herself no time for second thoughts and dithering, Annie turned around and unclipped Katie's seat belt. Katie's whimper cut right to the bone. "Come on, punkin," Annie whispered. "I promise you, everything will be fine." She swallowed the fear rising inside.

Everything *would* be fine. She'd make it fine. Rubbing her eyes, Annie snagged her purse and rolled up the windows. She locked her door and slid out on the passenger side, scooting Will before her.

Will and Katie climbed out of the car and waited quietly on the grassy edge while Annie took the boxes that had been in the back seat and worked them in among the boxes and suitcases in the trunk.

Finally, she slammed shut the trunk lid and locked the passenger door. Gazing at her pinch-faced twosome, Annie reviewed her choices one last time. None of the options were wonderful.

She leaned down and swung Katie up and onto her shoulders. Katie's rag doll dangled from her hand. "Okay. Let's go, guys." Taking Will's slight hand, Annie superstitiously chased away the thought that this time, truly, things couldn't get worse.

"I don't like this," Will mumbled, moving as close as he could and looking around. Something rustled in the underbrush near them, and he stepped closer. Fog shifted around them and a drift of breeze wrapped her skirt around Will, cocooning him in fabric. "Maybe we should stay here."

Tugging gently, Annie stepped forward. "This doesn't seem to be a very busy road, Will, or we would." Watching his distressed expression, Annie started to change her mind and stuff them all back into the car behind locked doors until morning.

A flick of green, half-seen from the corner of her eye.

Puzzled, she turned. Gone. But this time she was certain she'd seen that green beckoning to her, calling her forward.

"It's too dark." Will pulled her hand. "We need a flashlight."

Annie stopped and carefully stooped to face her son who slept with a night-light on and wouldn't go into a dark room alone. "Will, I saw some kind of light up there." She pointed, and he looked in the direction she indicated. "I think there's a gas station or restaurant up ahead. We'll only go that far, okay? We'll be able to find help there."

Reluctantly, he nodded, still not liking the idea even with the provisions she'd added. "Maybe it will be closed."

"Maybe so." Annie stood up. "But it's only nine." She sighed. "Please, Will, try not to worry."

He didn't respond. In a viselike grip, he held her hand and walked beside her. His small, thin body felt warm through the fabric of her skirt.

They walked away from the car, their feet making shushing sounds against the tough grass and sand. All around them the rumbling chorus of bullfrogs sang to them through the fog-clouded dark.

Once Will turned around and looked back. "I can't see our car." His voice was low and frightened in the alien landscape, his body rigid and tense as he glued himself to her side.

For a long time they walked, the children silent, Katie sometimes walking, sometimes asking to be carried, Annie trying to see through the bewildering gray.

Then, suddenly, through a shift of fog, green winked on and off. Annie shifted Katie's weight in her arms for a moment.

"I seed the green light," Katie whispered, brushing her cheek against the top of Annie's head. "S'there. Really."

Something about Katie's certainty sent Annie's panic swirling away like storm water down a drain.

"Me, too. I saw it," Will added, his tense frame relaxing.

Maybe because it was Christmas, maybe because she was at heart an optimist, but for the life of her, Annie couldn't explain the sense of peace that gradually crept into her as she and the children trudged steadily through the damp fog toward that light flickering on and off before them, leading them on through the darkness.

Off to the right of the road, a spurt of red interrupted the occasional green flickers and Annie stopped so abruptly, Katie's chest bumped against the back of her mother's head as they looked where Will was pointing.

"Look! It's a star," Will said. "A sign!"

Behind a concealing thicket of live oaks and pines, a red-and-green, five-pointed star blinked on and off over the roof of a squat building seeming to float in the fog. Most of the lights in the sign were burned out, but as Annie watched, a red neon section sputtered into life and died, leaving one lone green point flickering on and off in the mist.

Five cars dotted the dark parking lot, and a dimly lit sign under the star proclaimed that they had arrived at the Star Inn.

Not a gas station. That was obvious. Secluded by untended bushes and trees, its lights half-extinguished, the Star Inn was about as inviting as the Bates Motel.

They'd followed the green light. They'd arrived at their destination.

Annie wondered if she should feel relieved.

But that strange sense of sureness and peace that she'd felt since the first moment she'd seen the flickering green light kept her feet moving toward the dark unwelcoming door of the Star Inn, made her reach out and turn the cold, greasy metal of the doorknob.

Night air eddied in slow currents over the smoke and low voices as the door opened.

But it was the silence after the door eased shut that had Ben looking up.

"What the hell?" Midswipe down the long mahogany length of his bar, Ben faltered.

The woman standing on the threshold of his bar looked as if she'd collapse in a heap if she took one more step. Even across the room he could see the faint tremble in her lower lip. Her small delicate frame swaying as she stood there, she lifted her rounded chin and surveyed the room as if she owned it. As she glanced at his lingering customers, the dim lights around the door caught in her thick, fog-dampened hair and turned its brown to gold-and-red shimmers.

She held the hand of a small boy, drawing him closer to her side as she checked out the room. The boy's other hand was wrapped firmly in the folds of her skirt, twisting it up on the side where a sliver of pale thigh glowed against the wine-red cotton and held Ben's gaze for a long moment.

He made himself look away from that pale strip of skin.

Nestled against the woman's narrow shoulder, the little girl in her arms twisted to face the room and caught Ben's scrutiny.

Her solemn, dark blue eyes never left his as he frowned.

Clearly not sure whether to step into the room or run for the hills, the woman stood with one narrow foot on the scarred floor, the other pressed back against the door.

Wishing her Godspeed to the hills, Ben frowned again, looking away as he made a vicious swipe against the polish of the wood bar, wiping away shallow pools of spilled liquor and ice.

Keeping his head down, he ran his fingertip along the wood. Stretching the length of one wall, the counter was the focal point of the room.

Shining, satin-smooth, not a nick or bump in the dark wood, glistening with undertones of red.

Like the woman's hair.

Reluctantly, Ben glanced again at the three of them.

The children looked as exhausted as the woman. The boy had that drawn, worried look kids got when they had to be adults too early.

He scrubbed hard at a sticky spot marring the gloss. Damn the woman. What was she doing dragging these kids into his bar, anyway?

A heavy thwack in his ribs interrupted his determined polishing. Ben scowled down at the top of Gabe's bald head. "Yeah? What?"

"Well, Ben, old son, looks like our Christmas angel done walked right down from the top of our tree and lit at our front door. That's what."

Scanning the bar where a solitary hula doll wiggled her light-festooned skirt, the sole concession he'd made to the season, Ben glared. "Not funny, old man."

God, he hated Christmas.

Always had. Always would.

"Reckon not," Gabe drawled. "But she's real pretty, even so. And them cherubs of hers—"

"They don't belong here. Hell, it's almost midnight."

"Only ten-fifteen, old son. Don't get your shorts in a knot." Gabe's smile was provokingly amiable.

"Whatever. It's way past bedtime for angels and cherubs. Don't they have school tomorrow, anyway?" Ben pulled the handle on the lager beer and watched the mug fill with froth and gold. "Get them out of here, Gabe." He slid the mug down the bar, his hard thrust leaving a trail of foam down the shining wood.

"Hell's bells, Ben. What snake bit you in the rear end?" Gabe scratched the line on his head where bald melded with curly gray.

Turning his back to Gabe's angel and cherubs, Ben smacked his open palm against the bar. "I want them out of here."

"I don't." Fists doubled against his skinny hips, Gabe stuck his bulldog chin out.

In the mirror facing him, Ben saw the woman and children edge to an empty table close to the door and sit down. The woman brushed the chair bottoms first with paper napkins from the table. He shook his head. "No kidding, Gabe. Take care of it. Or I will."

"Right. A trio of real troublemakers, all right. Anybody could see that right off. No wonder you want them off the premises." Gabe rolled his eyes and shot a look toward the table where the boy sat close to the woman. "Hell, the boy looks like he could tear this place apart with one hand tied behind his back."

"You going to make me tell them to hit the road?" Ben didn't raise his voice. "You know I will." He didn't want to look at the worry-pinched face of that boy, didn't want to see the woman's vulnerable exhaustion every time he looked up from the bar. "I don't want them in my bar. Period."

His chin quivering pugnaciously, Gabe glared at him with faded blue eyes. "My bar, too, Ben."

"You want to buy me out, old man?" Ben stepped back, the itchy hostility he'd felt from the moment the woman and children walked in finally finding an outlet. "Fine. No sweat. I can be history by tomorrow. Say the word." Crossing his arms, he leaned back against the bar and waited for Gabe's answer.

Whenever Ben wanted, he could pick up and leave. That had always been part of their agreement. Question was, he wondered, as belligerence settled back to that nagging itchiness, did he want Gabe to call him on his threat?

Watching Gabe's watery old eyes, Ben wasn't sure any more why he'd been so hair-triggered.

Even so, he wasn't about to back down. Irritable with himself, he shifted uneasily.

His four years working the Star Inn had set some kind of longevity record. When the old proverbial push came to shove, fact was, he liked the run-down joint.

Still waiting for Gabe's reply, Ben watched the mirror where the reflections of the reds and browns and gold of the stacked up liquor bottles mingled into a muted glow. And in the middle of that mirrored kaleidoscope, the woman's thick hair swung against her throat like a lover's hand, a slow, sliding stroke, as she bent toward the boy.

In the mirror behind the bar Gabe's gaze met his. And saw too much.

His hands dropping to his sides, Ben looked away. Damn the old man.

After a long pause, Gabe finally said, "I'll go see what they want." His rough hand hovered in the vicinity of Ben's shoulder. "No reason me and you should be fighting."

"No reason at all." Ben's throat was tight, and his tone was rougher than he'd meant, but Gabe nodded and ambled away, the seat of his pants droopy around his skinny butt.

Reaching down, Ben snagged a bottle of beer. Still watching in the mirror, he popped off the cap. As the cap clattered and rolled around his feet, he watched the woman smile at Gabe.

Gabe was right.

If angels smiled, it would look like that, filled with warmth and light, a smile that transformed into radiance that dim corner of the bar where she sat.

Against the constriction in his throat, Ben took a long swallow of icy beer and stared in the mirror. There, in the dark reflection of wooden tables and chairs, in the brown-and-gold shimmer of bottles, the woman's smile glowed like a distant star.

For a long moment, he stared. Like a cold winter surf, loneliness backwashed through him.

Then, tilting the bottle, he swallowed again and turned away, thumping the bottle onto the counter. He had a sink filled with glasses to be washed and wiped. He picked up a long, tulip-shaped beer glass. Gabe would see the woman on her way.

Or he would himself.

Ben glanced up, straight into the judgmental eyes of the frowning boy. The woman's hand curved protectively around his neck, and her head tilted to the side as she laughed at something Gabe had said, her hair swinging back from the column of her slim throat. The little girl toyed with the button at the neck of the woman's rose-colored blouse, working the top button in and out of its buttonhole. Watching each slip and slide of the tiny button, Ben felt his fingers burn.

The woman glanced at him, her face still soft with laughter. Sudsy water dripped down his wrists and onto his shoes. He meant to look away from the delicate curve revealed at the edge of the buttonhole, but he didn't.

Catching the direction of his gaze, the woman stilled the child's restless play by placing her palm over the toddler's twining fingers, but one childish finger hooked in the open neck of the woman's blouse and heat rose under Ben's skin as he watched the small finger curl against the woman's breast.

A slow tide of pink swept up the woman's neck and into her face as she stared back at Ben, her rosy mouth still half-parted in laughter, her eyes under the winging brown eyebrows wide and startled.

Warmth and a kind of innocence in those guileless eyes smiling at him.

The glass shattered in his hand.

Sparkles of glass diamond-dusted the floor and sink counter. Ben eased a shard free from the pad of his thumb and bent to pull out a whisk broom and dustpan from the cabinet next to the sink.

Pressing his finger hard against the bead of blood forming at the base of his hand, he rested his forehead against the cabinet door.

He knew trouble when it walked in through his front door. Every instinct he'd ever trusted at the most primitive level of his being screeched out loud and clear: *trouble*.

Paying attention to his instincts was second nature by now. He would use whatever passed for his brains these days and keep himself damned busy and out of sight until Gabe's angel left.

Whisking up the splinters, he dumped them into the trash, carefully avoiding glances at the table in the corner near the front door.

The sting of the hot water against the cut kept him focused.

Even when Gabe came back to the grill and slapped down three hamburgers, smashing the buns flat with the long spatula, Ben kept his mouth shut. He'd spoken his piece.

Anyway, the loneliness the woman had stirred in him was none of Gabe's damned business.

Gabe, of course, nosy old coot that he was, made it his business. "Them three got problems."

Not answering, Ben ran his finger around the edge of the wet mug until it sang, the high-pitched note clear and pure over the muffled noises in the smoky bar. He scrubbed against a purple lipstick smudge on the edge of a tumbler. The woman's mouth had been wide and full, her soft pink lips parted as she laughed.

"Car broke down. Stranded 'em a ways back." Gabe flipped the meat patties. Grease sizzled on the grill.

Looking at him sideways, Ben said, "So? Not my concern. Not yours, either, old man."

"Good will toward men and Merry Christmas to you, too." Gabe slammed the spatula down and turned to glare at him. "Who's goin' to come out tonight and fix their car? Huh? What do you think they're going to do, that angel and her kiddies?" Gabe and grease sputtered in a harmony of hissing and spattering.

"Yeah? Make your point," Ben muttered.

"Think about it, you mule-headed rock," Gabe growled. "Woman and her two kids. Stranded out here in the middle of nowhere." Swiveling back to the grill and ignoring the mutters coming from the mule-headed rock, he slipped the patties onto the bun bottoms and plunked four pickles on top of each thick meat patty. Stabbing red-and-green plastic-topped toothpicks into the center of each hamburger with righteous intensity, he cleared his throat as if he was about to speak and then changed his mind.

The old man's back was articulate with accusation. Looking at that rigid spine, Ben felt his stomach spasm.

The hairs on the back of his neck spiked in alarm. He knew what was coming.

"Where they gonna go, huh? This time of night?" Gabe stacked three plates on one arm and grabbed a ketchup bottle with his other hand. "And bring two milks and a cola over to their table."

"You're pushing too hard, old man." Ben yanked a bottle of milk from the refrigerator and poured two glasses. Milk slopped onto his hands and he swore under his breath.

Not looking at him, Gabe shuffled off, his stooped shoulders hunched protectively around the plates. "Shut up and bring the drinks, Ben. It won't kill you to act like a human being for a change instead of like a grizzly bear woke up from hibernation."

Standing next to the rickety table and looking down at the shining gold-brown of the woman's hair, Ben's sympathies were all for the grizzly. Edging the drinks in front of the woman and children, he stepped back, ready to beat a fast retreat behind the bar.

Gabe caught the edge of his shirt, stopping him. "This here's Ben Jackson, my partner. Ben, Annie Conroy. And Will and Katie."

Ben folded his arms and nodded at the two solemn kids, his glance lingering for a moment on the thin-faced boy and his square, stubborn chin. Different in shape, the boy's chin was as stubborn as the mother's gently rounded one. Reluctantly, Ben looked up from that delicate stubbornness right into Annie Conroy's eyes.

His heart bumped once, hard, and then slowed, but he could hear the slow pulse thudding in his ears.

He'd known she would be trouble.

Underneath the sweetness and the smiles, he saw the vulnerability in those smoky-blue depths, a vulnerability that tugged at him in spite of all his instincts to ignore it. He saw, and didn't want to, the fatigue in her pale, oval face and in the faint tremble at the edge of her soft mouth. He saw, too, the panic hovering at the edge of those eyes looking hopefully up at him.

Oh, Gabe was wrong, wrong, wrong. This could kill him, one way or another.

"Hello, Mr. Jackson," Annie Conroy said, and her voice was like wind chimes on a lazy afternoon. She extended her slim hand to him. "Mr. Thibideaux said you could help us."

"Yeah?" Ben glanced from beneath lowered lids to Gabe and uttered a flat, uncompromising expletive under his breath. "He did, did he?" Not taking Annie Conroy's small hand in his, Ben saw the hope in her bright face fade as she glanced, puzzled, at her outstretched hand before letting it fall to her lap.

She frowned, the smooth, dark brown eyebrows drawing together in embarrassment. "Perhaps he was wrong?" She controlled the music of her voice, making it friendly, easy and unconcerned, but the effort pitched the last syllable higher.

Ben heard the strain that betrayed her attempt to appear calm. Heard it and, listening to his instincts, forced himself to ignore it.

His arms still folded across his chest, Ben said, "He was wrong. I can't help you."

"I see." One finger dug at the center of her hamburger. "Of course. I understand. Really, I do." She looked up at him and smiled, her fingers poking a row of holes all around the edge of the hamburger bun, crumbs raining onto the plate.

Watching that downpour of bread crumbs, Ben saw, way back in the depths of her smoky eyes, hope, like a candle flame, flicker and die.

But he didn't speak, not even when Gabe kicked him.

She plucked one last piece of bread and rolled it between her fingers. "Well, thanks, anyway." She nudged the children's plates closer to them. "Go ahead, guys. Start eating. These are great burgers."

And then she looked one last time at him.

Gone, that last gleam of hope in her glowing face, and Ben thought for a moment that the corner of the room suddenly seemed darker and colder.

Chapter Two

Staring into Ben Jackson's unfriendly hazel eyes, Annie knew she'd sooner crawl across burning lava than ask this man for help. The open hostility in his square face indicated he'd probably let her, too.

Earlier, laughing, she'd turned her head and seen him staring at her reflection in the mirror with that same wary animosity. It wasn't the animosity, though, that had captured her gaze, held it and filled her face with heat.

Lurking behind Ben Jackson's heavy-lidded hostility, hunger, naked and all-male, had stared at her from the mirror.

And she hadn't been able to tear her eyes from that lonely hunger, something deep in her feminine nature responding to it.

Blindly, Annie tore off a piece of bun and chewed it.

"Damn it to hell and back, Ben," Gabe growled.

The white of Ben's shirt was ghostly in the shadows of the bar, a wavering presence before her as he moved and then was still, his impassive stance charged and resonating with reined-in emotions. "I told you before, drop it, old man."

"Damned if I will, you pigheaded, gator-brained stump. I promised her you'd help."

"You shouldn't have made promises you can't keep. You know what I said." Unmoved, keeping his voice low, Ben Jackson surveyed his partner.

Annie rubbed her aching forehead, trying to sort out her thoughts in the midst of chaos.

"You've gone too far this time, Ben. I—" The old man's voice slowed to a halt, and the silence grew uncomfortable.

In a part of her mind that functioned in spite of this latest disaster, Annie heard Gabe Thibideaux's angry words. She rolled a pellet of bread and swallowed it, the bread sticking in her throat.

She wouldn't cry, not in front of Katie and Will. She couldn't do that to them. They'd placed their faith in her. If she broke down, they'd see all their security vanishing with each of her tears. She swallowed another pellet.

The silence between them lengthened awkwardly. Gabe finally resumed speaking, his voice tired and querulous, anger draining from him and giving way to resignation. "I don't think I can find it in my heart to forgive you for this, Ben."

Annie heard their words from the far end of the tunnel she'd fallen into.

The younger man shifted his weight. He'd strolled over in a stride as smooth and powerful as a river of molten steel, and Annie had been able to take a deep breath for the first time since leaving the nursing home.

There was competence and power in his walk, rock-steady stability in the cut of his short brown hair scraped severely back from his hard face. Despite the rebellious wave of one thick strand back from his broad forehead, it was the haircut of a man who didn't given a damn for current fashion.

She could imagine him walking into a barbershop and ordering, "Short. Nothing fancy."

That stability and the strength implied by Ben Jackson's wide-shouldered body and his muscular arms had eased the tightness in her chest. Relief filling her, she'd smiled up at him like the sun coming up after a long night.

More fool, she, she thought as she watched the restless movement of his polished shoes. Spit-shined shoes didn't belong in a bar like this. In the formality of his neatly creased slacks and white shirt with its rolled up sleeves, Ben Jackson was out of place.

Glancing up at his mouth clamped shut in anger and his shuttered face, she had the strangest impression that this man would seem out of place anywhere, rootless.

Like her, in fact, at the moment.

Sliding Katie's glass of milk closer to the girl, Annie glanced away from the two angry men. A strange argument, with one furious voice and one seething silence, she thought numbly.

She should have learned. She'd certainly had enough lessons to last a lifetime. But for a few minutes, listening to the casual teasing of Gabe Thibideaux, she'd forgotten everything she'd taught herself. In those seconds, the scrawny old man and his muscular partner had loomed as formidable in her mind as any mythic knight ever had to any fair lady.

But she'd learned slowly and painfully that the only knight on a charger she could count on for rescue was herself.

And if sometimes the armor grew heavy and unwieldy and the quest impossible, tough. Protecting her kids was still her job, nobody else's.

"You've gone over the line, Ben, no matter what—" Gabe was plucking futilely at the waist ties of his apron.

Annie caught the way Ben jammed his arms tighter under his armpits as he drawled, "I don't like people making promises for me. You know that, Gabe."

Ben Jackson might present an impenetrable mask to the world, but Gabe had scratched that indifferent surface, and Annie glimpsed, but didn't understand, the pain that flashed and vanished for that unguarded instant in the depths of Ben's hazel eyes.

"Old man," he said with a sigh, his fists doubling under his arms, "don't paint me into a corner. I don't like it. And it won't work."

"Seems to me you're the one done painted yourself into the corner. Nobody else." Gabe shrugged, defeated.

Watching Will lick the milky mustache off his mouth, Annie knew she had only one course of action. The spark of hope she'd felt as Ben Jackson had walked over to her had died. Fighting back the treacherous panic clawing for a permanent foothold in her chest, she rubbed her forehead.

She and the children could walk back to the car. Gabe had already told her the nearest gas station was thirty miles farther south and not open after nine at night. She would ask Gabe to call the station and arrange for a tow first thing in the morning. By the time Will and Katie woke up, the tow truck would be there.

It would be a long night, but tomorrow, with the sun burning away the shadowy fog along the highway and in her brain, they would be all right.

She was tired, that's all. Things would look better in the morning, in the sunshine.

Fumbling in her purse, she pulled out several singles and change. "How much do I owe you, Mr. Thibideaux?" She laid the bills on the table and finally took a bite of her burger. "It's delicious," she said automatically, forcing the food down but tasting nothing.

Surprised, the two men scrutinized her for an uncomfortable minute before the older one spoke, biting off his words, "How much does she owe, Ben? Huh? Make sure you charge her for large milks, not small ones, and, oh, be sure she pays for the extra napkins, okay?"

In that tense moment, only Annie's need to leave the Star Inn without falling apart and embarrassing herself kept her upright, talking like a tape on fast advance and pretending that everything was peachy-keen. "Really special hamburger." She took another bite and swallowed.

She'd never taken charity in her life. Couldn't, wouldn't, not after everything she'd done to keep her family's leaky boat afloat. And now anger of her own made her toes and fingertips buzz, her ears hum. Not wanting Ben Jackson with his forbidding face to know the full extent of her desperation, she smiled at Gabe Thibideaux. "If you'd call the tow truck for me tomorrow, I'd appreciate it." Anger uncurling up from her toes and energizing her, driving her headlong into foolhardiness, she unfolded several singles, adding an extra dollar as pride and reckless anger made her declare, "I left money to cover the cost of the call." She smiled again as sweetly as she knew how, the muscles along her jaw stretching painfully, and risked a sideways glance at Ben Jackson as she rose and dropped her bunched up napkin beside her plate.

His frown satisfied her pride.

Shutting everything out except the need to reach the front door and get outside, Annie pushed her chair under the table and reached for Katie and Will. Lifting Katie into her arms, she pushed the door ajar with her right hand and stepped out into the cool night.

Leaving the warmth and noise of the Star Inn behind her, she shut the door with her fanny.

The still-foggy night wove threadily around her ankles in the almost-empty parking lot.

Peace.

But no refuge.

She'd crossed her bridges, burned all of them behind her and left herself without a boat or an oar. Gulping the fresh air as tears threatened, she wanted to laugh at her stupid pride and found instead she couldn't get enough air into her lungs, couldn't stop the gasping noises, a cross between laughter and tears, that rolled up from her stomach, shivering and shaking her until her teeth chattered.

"Mommy?" Katie patted her cheek. "Mommy cold?" Her tiny fingers tapped Annie's shaking lips.

"Leave Mommy alone, Katie." Will tugged at Katie's hand.

"No, it's okay, Will. Everything's fine," Annie finally gasped out. "Some of my hamburger went down my windpipe. That's all." She stroked Will's cheek, and for what surely must be the millionth time in his short life, added, "Don't worry."

"Ahmadilla," Katie suddenly whimpered desperately.

"Heavens, how could we have forgotten her?" Annie whispered through the laughing, sobbing gulps choking her.

Katie had named the homemade rag doll Armadillo because she'd liked the sound of the word in a story Will had read to her late one night.

Katie never went anywhere without Armadillo.

"But we can't go back inside," Annie said, every bit as exhausted and desperate as Katie. She couldn't return to the Star Inn and face Ben Jackson twice in one night.

"Ahmadilla." Katie's forlorn plea hung in the still, misty night.

"Oh, Katie-love, I can't go get your dolly," Annie murmured into the crease of her daughter's sweet-smelling neck.

"Ahmadilla *needs* me." Katie's voice quavered. "And *I* need her. Please, Mommy." Katie's neck was hot and damp with her silent, salty tears.

From the Star, muted sounds of laughter drifted to them outside under the pine trees.

Inside, contemplating the door that had been quietly shut in his face, Ben still saw Katie's head drooping against her mother's shoulder, still saw Annie Conroy's sweetly false smile that wobbled across her pale face and never reached her eyes.

But it was the censure he'd seen in her son's old-young eyes that twanged at his shriveled conscience. He shouldn't give two hoots in hell for the condemnation he'd seen in the kid's face.

And he didn't.

But he kept looking at the door, half expecting Annie and her kids to walk back in. When the door stayed closed, he swiveled to Gabe, startled to find him at the bar, his apron off.

Gabe folded his apron and placed it on the gleaming wood. He slumped back against the rolled edge of the bar as he spoke. "I don't understand you. I sure as shooting thought I did, but I don't, I reckon. I thought we were friends."

"You know we are." Watching Gabe's listless movements, Ben frowned.

"Yeah? Friends ought to be able to count on each other, not get shot down." He shuffled to the storage closet in the storeroom at the back of the bar and took down his windbreaker. "What you did tonight goes beyond ornery, Ben. I thought better of you, old son." The disappointment in Gabe's weary old voice twanged right along with Annie Conroy's son's accusation, a noisy jangling Ben tried to ignore.

His hands curling inside his pockets, Ben shrugged. There was nothing he could say to excuse his behavior. He couldn't explain to Gabe why he'd behaved the way he had. Since he didn't understand his behavior himself, how in hell could he make Gabe understand? Or forgive? Ben shrugged again.

"I'm gonna go get my truck and give them a ride down to Azalea Park. I don't know when I'll get back. I may decide to stay there over Christmas. Don't know if I feel like spending my holiday with a horse's hind end."

"You can't drive at night." Ben smoothed his damp palms down his slacks while he watched Gabe struggle with the sleeves of his jacket. "You can't see two feet in front of you, old man. You haven't driven at night in the four years I've known you." He smoothed his palms again and walked toward the bar, Gabe's sluggish movements concerning him.

"Well, the angel can drive then. But I'm not leaving them to walk down that road again tonight." Gabe couldn't get the zipper end of his jacket into the track. "Hell." He coughed.

The old man's phlegmy cough was one more accusation in Ben's ears.

Gently bumping the gnarled hands aside, Ben eased the tab onto the track. "All right. You win. I'm a horse's hind end. But I never pretended I wasn't, old man. You know that." He stepped back, letting Gabe finish zipping up the jacket. "I'll go get the pickup." Ben slammed the door on all the instincts roaring in his mind.

"You sure?" Gabe scowled at him.

"Hell, no." Ben lifted one shoulder. "All I'm sure of is that I'm the biggest idiot in the state for giving in to you. You'll never let me live it down. Every time you don't get your way, I know how it'll be. You'll threaten to get behind the wheel of the truck." Ben shook his head. "I know damned certain I'm making a mistake letting you con me like this."

Gabe's smile was tinged with mockery. "I figure you'll survive."

And when Ben opened the door of the bar and saw the trio huddled under the pine tree, heard Katie's muffled sobs, saw Annie Conroy's shoulders slumped in defeat as she half turned back to the Star, he knew, oh, he knew he was making the biggest mistake of his life letting Annie and her children anywhere near him.

And looking at Will's defensive glare, Ben wanted to strangle Gabe Thibideaux with his bare hands.

Would have, too, if the old fool hadn't had the sense to stay in the bar.

"Mommy." Will's hand pulled hard at the woman's skirt.

"What?" Her round chin was lifted skyward, her voice haughty, but the huskiness of her choked-back tears ruined the effect. Shifting and glowing in the fog, her wine-red skirt rippled around her legs.

He couldn't get over the way she seemed to gleam with light even in the fog.

Even though he couldn't hide the reluctance roughing his words, Ben nodded as Will pointed at him. "I can give you a ride back to your car. You can get your suitcases. I'll drive you to the next town."

When her lips pursed and tightened, Ben knew she wanted nothing more than to throw his offer slap-back in his face.

Fact was, he wished she would.

But she didn't say anything while she examined him as if he were something she wanted to scrape off the bottom of her shoe.

He tried to ignore a voice in his head snidely telling him that there wouldn't be anything open in Azalea Park. His gut clenched as he peered at his watch. Not now. Hell, it was almost midnight.

Trouble. Oh, hell, yes, he'd known Annie Conroy was going to be trouble the first minute he'd seen her. He'd hoped he could stay out of her way, but like death and taxes, some things were inevitable.

And it looked like helping Annie Conroy and her kids was inevitable.

Ben shivered. Rolling down his sleeves, he buttoned his cuffs and strolled over to Annie Conroy, the lump of faded cloth he'd spotted on Katie's chair held in front of him like a shield.

Katie's dark blue eyes opened wide. "Ahmadilla! You found her!" From the security of Annie's arms, Katie tilted toward him, her arms outstretched.

"I saw it. Thought you might want it." He handed Katie the raggedy thing. The little girl's hand was cold as it brushed his.

He hadn't recognized that it was a doll. He didn't even know why he'd picked up the knobby object. He'd seen it and reached down, not thinking, only reacting.

Katie's face was buried somewhere in the middle of the rumpled doll.

Annie blinked. Then, those smooth eyebrows drawing together in a frown, she snugged Katie closer. "Thank you."

Ben knew she didn't want to take anything from him, didn't want to thank him and had done so only because of her child. "Do you still want a ride?"

The sag of relief in her slim body was visible even in the dark. "Yes, thank you," she repeated, and in her husky voice Ben heard the echo of her daughter's childish one as she'd seen the ragged toy in his hand. "You're very kind," she added.

"Kind?" Ben's laugh was mocking. He couldn't help it. "Don't count on it."

"No, I won't." There was no answering laughter in Annie Conroy's weary face. "I haven't counted on very much for a long time."

"Smart lady." Ben jiggled his keys in his pocket. "Saves a lot of grief."

"Sometimes." The slump in her narrow shoulders was more pronounced. But then she shrugged and a faint humor lifted the corners of her tender mouth. The humor then finally reached her eyes. "Not as much fun, though. The nineties woman. We can do it all. And with one hand tied behind our backs."

Her smile widened as she looked down at both her hands clasped tightly around her daughter. "Thank you, Mr. Jackson, for the offer of a ride, no matter how much you'd rather keep your distance from me and my problems. I'm grateful." Gently teasing, looking up at him from under lowered lashes, she finished, "And you don't have to worry. I promise I won't *count* on you."

Clearing his throat, Ben started to say something, anything, but she'd made it clear that she'd understood the argument between him and Gabe, knew that the only reason Ben was standing in front of her had nothing to do with *niceness* but everything to do with the old man. Instead, he pulled his keys out of his pocket and gestured with his head to the dark blue pickup in the darker shadows at the side of the bar.

An unwelcome regret stirred inside as he stalked to the truck, Annie and her children following him. Her candid acknowledgment of his motives had thrown him off balance.

She should have played the game, said thank-you, ignored all the undertones of the incident and pretended along with him that the situation was simple, ordinary.

But by letting him know she recognized his cynical unfriendliness, Annie Conroy had made it personal. And very complicated.

He wasn't surprised.

Katie clung to her mother's neck as Annie tried to climb into the cab of the pickup, so Ben muttered, "Sorry," and closed his hands around Annie's slim waist and boosted her into the truck.

Her waist was so narrow that his wide palms rose past her waistband and up against the light cotton of her pink blouse. Through the thin material, her ribs moved against his fingers as he held her, delicate, small bones covered by warm woman-skin and that cotton so silky-smooth he imagined he could feel each pore of her warm, pale skin.

He jerked his hands away, and, head down, Annie scooted into the cab. He couldn't look at her, not with the imprint of her waist and ribs burning the skin of his palms.

Hoisting Will up beside her and slamming the door, Ben walked around the back of the truck. The sudden craving to

feel Annie Conroy's warm, smooth skin beneath his hands
spiked through him, hot and painful. Unwanted.

The thin cotton of her blouse was a poor substitute, un-
satisfactory, for the silky heat he'd sensed underneath.

Cursing Gabe, Ben kicked the truck tire as hard as he
could.

The cab light came on, and before Annie quickly averted
her face, Ben saw the flush along her cheeks.

Damn Gabe to hell and back. Turning the key, Ben muttered, "Buckle up."

"Sure. Come on, guys." Shifting and adjusting the seat
belts around Will, pulling the middle one around Katie in
her lap and herself, Annie bumped Ben, her thigh sliding
along his as she turned.

Running his palms over the cool, slick plastic of the
steering wheel, Ben waited, his eyes shut, a red darkness
behind his eyelids, the flower-scent of Annie Conroy's
shampoo mixing with the piney coolness of the foggy night.

"Okay?" Ben looked out the windshield.

"We're all set. Thank—" She stopped. She brushed her
hair back from her face and that clean scent drifted to him.
"You know where the car is?"

"Hell, down the road until we find it, right?" The situation was impossible. He didn't understand anything that was
happening to him, didn't want to, only wanted to be back at
the bar with Annie Conroy somewhere far, far away, not
sitting next to him in the dark where every breath he took
was filled with her fragrance.

With Katie settled on Annie's lap, he knew the cab was
plenty big enough for the four of them, but he sensed the
movements of Annie's slight body as she stirred next to him.
Her shoulder shifted as she murmured something to Will,
her hip curved as she settled Katie more comfortably, her
breasts rose against her blouse as she sighed.

But she never actually brushed against him during the
entire drive back to her car. The foot-wide space between

them remained unbroached. The sensation of touching her was all in his head.

Maybe in hers, too, he decided crankily as he began to watch her carefully from the corner of his eye.

She was too conscientious about keeping that space between them. The distance between them stayed so even, she might as well have taken a ruler out and measured it. Nothing casual in her failure to make conversation, nothing casual about her careful avoidance of him even as she shifted in response to her children's murmurs and low questions.

Images of Annie and the children walking down the dark, empty road flashed in and out of Ben's brain as he drove past moss-shrouded, dripping trees, past shadowy undergrowth thick and forbidding along the road edge.

With each mile, that sense of inevitability he'd felt earlier grew heavier, a weight he tried to fight back each time he pushed away an image of Annie carrying Katie all that way in her arms, Will trudging beside them in the fog.

They would have been frightened.

"Damn," he muttered, hitting the steering wheel.

Annie jumped. "What is it?"

"Nothing. Sorry." He risked a full look at her.

Katie was asleep in Annie's arms, and Annie's own eyelids drooped as he watched. He didn't know how she could still be sitting upright, so how the hell was he going to send her and the kids down to Azalea Park with her half-asleep on her feet?

He'd get her car started and follow her to Azalea. Nodding, he relaxed. He could do that, see them safely down this stretch of road. There would be someplace for them to stay in the town.

One way or another, he'd find them a motel room in Azalea Park even if he had to tear the town apart.

Easing the truck off the road onto the sand and grassy edge, he bumped slowly over the rough ground until the truck and car were bumper to bumper. If he were lucky,

Annie Conroy's car would need nothing more than a jumped battery.

He reached past Annie and snicked open the glove compartment, fumbling inside for the heavy black flashlight. His knee slid past hers, and the whisper of mated fabric was as loud to his ears as a gunshot.

And the click of the cab door wasn't nearly as loud as the hiss of his slacks against her skirt. Holding the overhead-light button down so that the light wouldn't wake up the kids, Ben murmured, "I'll hook up the battery cables. That's the obvious problem. That or an empty gas tank."

Her raised eyebrows told him what she thought of his empty gas tank theory.

"Well, I didn't think it would be that easy." Swinging the flashlight by his side, thinking, Ben stared at her in the darkness. "You start your engine when I nod. All right?"

Annie nodded and slipped Katie onto the seat next to Will, where Katie drew her knees up to her chin and complained sleepily around her plugged-in thumb. Annie scooted out behind Ben, her skirt catching on the corner of the seat. "Drat," she whispered, groping for the fabric in back of her.

Nothing had gone right for him all night long. Why should things change? Ben bent past her, his shoulder steady against hers, her breathing a small sigh against his neck as he snaked his finger under the hem of her skirt and freed it.

Not for any amount of money would he have touched her at that instant, not with the feel of her warm breath lingering along the side of his neck and the silence and darkness close around them.

He stepped away too quickly, his finger slipping off the light button, and in the bright flash as Annie exited, she stumbled, her hand outstretched for balance, skimming his chest and catching on his belt buckle.

Everything happened so fast, her stumbling, the soft graze of her hand against his chest that he couldn't control the leap of response, the heavy beat of his blood. Couldn't control it but didn't want it.

Not with Annie Conroy.

Steadying herself, her hand dropping to her side, she stepped back as quickly as he had, her mouth a soft O, her eyes wide and dilated in the cab light.

Katie slept on, a curled up nugget on the seat, but, not surprisingly, Will came to full alert. "You can fix our car?"

Ben nodded. "I'm going to jump the battery."

An almost imperceptible shake of Will's head indicated his skepticism. Clearly, Will wasn't destined to become a member of Ben's fan club. Will didn't take anything on faith.

Wondering why he should feel insulted by the kid's lack of faith, Ben said, "Hand me the cables under your seat, will you?"

"Okay." The boy's voice was laced with discouragement as he pulled out the jumper cables. "Not the battery, I bet."

"Will!" Annie's whispered admonition didn't stop her son.

"Skeeter said distributor." A stubborn set to Will's chin as he leaned against the passenger door. "And Skeeter knows cars. Especially ours." He concluded with a frown at Ben, "You don't."

"That's enough, William Christian Conroy."

"I am telling the truth. Skeeter *does* know our car."

"Mr. Jackson's trying to help us. Apologize to him at once." No butter in Annie Conroy's even tones, no room for compromise in her quiet order.

Standing in the damp air, Ben held the cables and waited, amused as he observed Will's struggle to frame his apology.

The boy's chin dipped and raised. "I'm sorry I was rude."

As apologies went, it was the work of a pint-size diplomat. Will had avoided conceding that Ben might know as much as Skeeter, the phantom mechanic.

"Fine." Ben shoved the flashlight under his arm and extended his hand to Will. "Apology accepted."

Closing the door behind him, he walked with Annie to her car. In spite of everything that made him itchy around her, he liked that she didn't try to make excuses for her son's behavior. The boy apologized, Ben accepted, and it was a closed issue.

Waiting for her to release the hood latch, Ben turned on the flashlight. Caught in the white halo, Annie Conroy with her gleaming hair and pink blouse was a porcelain figurine, smooth and shining, fragile.

Breakable.

Ben turned the light away from her and onto the patchy ground where it filtered through the fog and onto the scuff mark on his shoe where he'd kicked the truck tire.

Annie Conroy was stripping away his control.

He'd see her on her way, and he'd be fine. It was Christmas. That was all.

He lifted the hood after she released the latch. He sighed as he saw the almost-new battery, but, hoping against hope, he hooked up the jumper cables between the two vehicles while Annie tried to start the car.

The futile cranking of the engine finally died as Annie turned off the engine.

Casting the flashlight beam over the engine as he checked plugs and wires, looking for obvious problems, Ben knew he wasn't going to be able to start Annie Conroy's car.

Will had been right to put his faith in Skeeter.

As Ben leaned over the engine, something bumped his calf, and he drew his head out from under the hood and shone the light down on Will's face, stark-white with misery.

"Maybe Skeeter was right." He bit his lip. "Maybe the module in the distributor."

Ben nodded. "Yeah. Maybe," he echoed.

"I hoped you could fix us," Will said, his mouth quivering. "What are we going to do now?"

Clicking off the light, Ben sighed. Good question. Unfortunately, he'd known the answer to it all along even though he'd tried to trick himself into believing otherwise. "Well, kid, you can't stay here."

Will's tiny exhalation of relief told Ben more than he wanted to know about the boy's worries and fears. "Maybe not," he agreed, looking around at the wildness of the dark landscape. "Maybe animals would come."

"No, you don't have to worry about animals." Not unless they were of the human variety, Ben amended to himself as he whacked the car hood down and stared at Annie's equally white and miserable face through the windshield.

Thank God Katie was asleep. He couldn't handle three miserable Conroys staring at him as if he were their last hope on earth.

He'd never wanted to be anybody's first, much less last hope.

The car door shut behind Annie, and Ben heard the swish of her skirt against a bush, the squeak of her shoes against grass and sand.

Damn, damn, and double-damn. Responsibility for Annie Conroy and her family weighed uncomfortably heavy on his shoulders. "Get your suitcases or whatever you'll need for a while. I'll drive you to Azalea Park."

"All right. Thanks. That's very kind of you." Annie's monotone and slump as she unlocked the trunk were testimony that she'd gone beyond exhaustion and worry to some twilight zone of numbness. Removing the suitcases she pointed to, Ben saw the packed boxes, the evidence of their lives crammed hurriedly into the trunk and on the floor of the back seat of the car.

In the silence as he and Will carried one big suitcase and a smaller one to the back of the truck, Ben decided that fate was out to get him.

No question about it, his name was definitely on the hit list of some malicious entity.

Yep, he had choices. In a pig's eye, he thought, opening the truck door and seeing Katie's small rump hunched against the back of the seat, her head pillowed on her doll.

Some choices all right.

He helped Will into the cab and backed away as Annie climbed in. Her own small rump was at his eye level as she ducked into the cab and cautiously lifted Katie. As they drove south, her cheek rested against Katie's flyaway hair, her arm curled tightly around her son, and if she shed a tear, Ben didn't want to see it.

The sweet fragrance drifting to him from her hair was torment enough.

Approaching the inn, he fought the impulse to turn off the road and into the Star where he belonged. The bar was closed and dark, the parking lot empty. Upstairs a light clicked off as they drove past, heading south to Azalea Park.

Next to him, Annie shifted tiredly, her head bouncing against Katie.

Will pressed his face to the window, staring at the deserted bar until it was behind them. He slid down onto his tailbone and huddled against the door.

The flickering neon star sputtered and winked for a long while in Ben's rearview mirror as he watched.

Red, green, green.

Red, green.

Gone.

And in the darkness of the rearview mirror, finally nothing but his own face staring bleakly back at him.

Chapter Three

Jolted awake, Annie clunked her head against Katie's. The truck had abruptly veered left.

Peering muzzily through the windshield for a glimpse of Azalea Park, Annie saw only wisps of fog trailing past the headlights. She looked toward Ben Jackson for an explanation. In the hissing of tires against the pavement, his stern profile was a silent silhouette of shadowed hollows and harsh planes.

"Mommy?" Katie nuzzled her forehead into Annie's arm.

Jaw cracking, Annie yawned, confused by the fog and dark. Stiff and sore, she felt as if she'd been sitting with her arms around Katie for hours, riding through the foggy dark with Ben Jackson some kind of grim presence at her side.

"Mommy?" More insistently the childish voice tugged at her awareness, bringing her fully awake.

"What, punkin?" Blinking and trying to assimilate the vague impressions jabbing her consciousness, Annie yawned again.

"Where are we, Mommy?" Katie rubbed her head under Annie's chin, her fine hair a tickle of silk against the sensitive underskin of Annie's chin.

"Mr. Jackson?" Even in the darkness, Annie saw the thin line of his mouth. Hesitantly, she tapped his arm. The muscled steel of his forearm bunched under her fingers, and she dropped her hand. "Where are we?"

"We're going back to the Star." His shirt sleeve was a hovering white line in the darkness, floating up and down as he rolled the steering wheel left, then right, bumping back onto the highway from a slickly executed revenuer's reverse.

At her side, Will made a small sound.

She hadn't seen the lights of any town. "We're returning? I don't understand."

Jagged and bitter, his laugh rasped along her spine and she shivered as he said, "Then that makes two of us because I'm damned if I understand, either, Annie Conroy."

It was the first time he'd used her name, but his quick grimace made it clear that he was annoyed with himself on several points, not the least of which was having slipped into even this much of a personal tone with her.

"Why aren't we going to Azalea Park?"

His long fingers rat-a-tat-tatted on the steering wheel. "I'm taking you and your kids to my place."

"You can't! I need to find a place for us to stay tonight. I have to make arrangements to have my car repaired," Annie finished wildly as visions of lurid headlines ran like ticker tape through her mind. "I have to repair my car! Let us out! Now!"

But Ben Jackson wasn't a seven-year-old boy used to obeying her. He didn't even lift his foot from the gas pedal.

"Stop, please." Fear made her mouth sand-dry. "Let us out."

"Why? You in the mood for a midnight hike down the road again?" Tat-a-tat-tat-a on the wheel.

"You're frightening Katie and Will," Annie whispered. "And me."

This time the truck slowed. "Sorry. I wasn't thinking." The frown he threw her way grooved deep vertical lines beside his thin, well-defined lips. "Yeah. Of course you were scared witless." The truck slowed to a sedate forty miles an hour.

"Not quite witless, I suppose," Annie said, managing a shaky smile.

"No?" He studied her face briefly while the truck droned forward.

She couldn't ever remember anyone who'd studied her with quite that same kind of intensity. His fleeting scrutiny pulled her out of herself, made her aware of the scrape of the truck seat along the backs of her knees, the pull of her blouse across her breasts.

And then he looked at the road, releasing her back into her own skin.

"Well, whatever you say." With one broad palm, he raked his fingers through his short hair, but it fell smoothly, tidily into place.

An orderly man, Ben Jackson. A man with a plan.

Thinking, Annie gently pushed Katie's hair from her face. Point one: Remembering the interchange between Ben and his partner, she knew she trusted Ben Jackson even though he was hostile, unfriendly and surly to the point of nastiness. He'd brought Katie her doll. Point two: For some reason, while she'd been asleep, he'd changed his mind about remaining aloof. Point three: He wasn't happy about having made that decision.

Where did that leave her and the children if she went along with whatever plan he'd made?

As the sliver of road streaked toward her through the mist, Annie wasn't sure she had a choice anymore.

Maybe she'd forfeited her choices once she'd stepped outside her car and walked down that bleached-out strip of pavement and stepped into Ben Jackson's run-down bar.

"What happens once we're back at the Star?" Annie laid her hand over Will's nervously jiggling leg.

"I don't know." Ben's tapping fingers matched the rhythm of Will's leg. "But by now, they've rolled the sidewalks up in Azalea Park." Grudgingly he said, "Gabe was right. You would have been stranded. I don't know what I was thinking of."

Annie didn't even try to restrain her chuckle. "You made your thoughts *very* clear, Mr. Jackson. You didn't want to be involved."

"Yeah." His restless tapping ceased. "I was a bastard. Gabe already read me the riot act."

A broken-bottle-topped, electrified fence instantly rose twenty feet tall and surrounded him.

Curiosity rippled under the surface of her thoughts. His withdrawal was so complete, she could almost hear the buzzing of the current through that imaginary barrier, but *something* had made him come after her, *something* had made him change his mind about abandoning them in Azalea Park before they'd even gotten to the town.

Curiosity made her want to climb over that glass-chunked fence, but she wasn't sixteen years old anymore and in the grip of the true-love myth. She no longer believed in the power of love to change someone who didn't want to be changed. What you saw was what you got.

Every time.

And a smart woman wouldn't fool herself into hoping differently.

Annie bolted the lid on the curiosity that made her wonder about the lonely hunger showing down deep in Ben Jackson's eyes, bolted the lid on all that dangerous curiosity and shoved it far away.

Lonely men with keep-away signs stuck all over them like sticky notes were best left alone.

But still...

She'd always had a sneaky sympathy for Pandora, who hadn't been able to control her curiosity, either.

Linking her arms around Katie, Annie braced them as Ben spun the truck into the Star's deserted parking lot and turned off the engine.

Maybe he intended for her and the kids to sleep in the truck, she decided as he opened the cab door and stepped out easily, his muscular thighs flexing and flowing in a physical and visual harmony she envied more than she'd admit as she climbed stiffly out of the truck and reached back for Katie.

Annie scanned the interior. They could sleep in the truck. It was possible. Not very comfortable, but possible. "What now?" she said, no longer having any clue about the motives behind Ben Jackson's actions.

The truck keys jingled as he pitched them up and down. "Gabe and I live here. Upstairs." Catching the keys at the apex of their glittering arc, he pointed, and Annie's gaze followed the sparkle of metal dangling from Ben Jackson's long fingers.

Away from the fitful gleam of the neon sign, a row of windows formed a second story along the short side of the building where it disappeared into the misty shadows of a stand of pines and dwarf cypress.

"You're offering us a place to stay?" Annie knew her mouth must have dropped to the floor of the truck.

"For tonight."

"Here?" She must have misunderstood. Surely Ben Jackson didn't intend to put himself out by the kind of offer she thought she'd heard.

"Yeah. Here. There isn't any other place. Not tonight."

"Why are you offering to help us? You didn't want to earlier. I can manage. Really," Annie insisted, uncomfortable down to the roots of her hair. Ben Jackson threw her off balance, looking at her as if he were touching her skin with his strong fingers, letting her know the whole time he didn't like her or her kids, and now he offered help when she'd never needed it more in her life.

It was definitely more blessed to give than to receive. Nobody liked having to be the grateful recipient of favors, especially grudgingly offered ones, and Ben Jackson's help was definitely grudging.

Her reluctant Good Samaritan quirked a thick eyebrow in the direction of Will, who was edging past his sister and toward Annie. "Your kids need a place to bunk down. They must be tired. I am. It's the middle of the night, and I'm right out of other choices." He offered rescue, but the ice crackling through his flat tones made his antipathy clear. Scraping his hands through his hair, he shrugged, but he didn't offer an apology for the undercurrent of coldness. His shrug said take-it-or-leave-it, he didn't give a damn one way or the other.

Waiting tigerlike, he was coiled and action-ready, his body language saying one thing, that flicker of something in his hooded eyes speaking a different language, the flicker sputtering and dying like the neon sign casting first red, now green shadows across the angles of his face.

It was a language Annie didn't have the time or energy to learn, no matter how much that glimpse of loneliness in this remote, reserved man tugged at her.

"Well, what do you want to do?" he repeated, his hip-shot stance pulling the trouser fabric tight across his flat stomach. Easy, relaxed, but the abrupt shift of one polished shoe scraping against the shell driveway betrayed him.

Patting Katie's back, Annie fought reality with pride even while she knew pride had no chance, not with Will wrapping himself in her skirt and Katie draped over her shoulder like a soggy noddle.

"We can't stand here in the fog until morning, Annie Conroy." Again his shoe scraped against the driveway.

"We don't know you. You don't know us. We're strangers to you."

"That's right. I could be an ax murderer, for all you know. You could be, too, as far as *I* know," he said, mockery shading his drawl.

"There has to be *some* place we can go, some other solution."

"Not one I could live with when the sun came up," he muttered, rolling his broad shoulders one after the other, the light fabric of his shirt moving loosely across his torso with each twist of his solid chest.

In her bone-weary exhaustion and confusion, desperately clinging to pride and so tired of fighting, Annie had an urge to lean on Ben Jackson's rock-hard chest and surrender, to let someone else cope for a while.

But she'd never leaned on anyone in all her life, and she wouldn't start now, especially not with Ben Jackson. If she leaned on him, he'd probably back away so fast, she'd wind up facedown in the shell parking lot.

Even in her drained confusion, Annie knew one truth for sure. She didn't want to be indebted to Ben Jackson.

Debts always had to be repaid.

"Mommy, I have to go to the bathroom," Will said, embarrassment and urgency in the jerk of his fist on her skirt.

"What's it going to be, Annie Conroy? The devil or the deep blue sea?" A trace of amusement in his low voice.

That amusement decided her. "The devil it is, then," she said, matching him taunt for taunt, somehow managing to make her voice as amused as his. "Come on, Will. Mr. Jackson's going to let us stay in his stable tonight."

"A stable? With horses? I don't understand. What do you mean?" Will dragged on her hand.

"Nothing, Will, nothing. I didn't mean anything. I was making a joke," Annie said, not daring to glance at the broad shadow of Ben Jackson strolling beside her.

"Not funny," Will grumbled, sounding like the seven-year-old he really was.

"No, punkin, it wasn't."

Glaring at her, Will dropped his death-hold on her skirt. "I'm your *boy*."

Punkin was all right for five-year-old Katie, but not for Will.

With Ben Jackson close at her side, Annie shifted Katie to her other shoulder and followed him across the parking lot, shells crunching beneath their feet in the late-night silence.

He opened a back door to the building, flipped on a light switch along the wall and waited for her to precede him into a ten-by-ten storeroom lined with cardboard boxes, rows of liquor bottles and cans of olives and pickles.

His unexpectedly old-fashioned manners went with his polished shoes and knife-creased slacks. However, she was more aware than she wanted to be of his tiger-energy cloaked by the veneer of his pressed slacks and polished shoes as he waited next to her, the heat of his solid body radiating to her in the close confines of the storeroom.

He was too close for her comfort, and she stepped away, her heart bumping fretfully.

It wasn't Ben Jackson's fault she sensed the tiger underneath. Her prickly awareness of his maleness was *her* problem, not his, she reminded herself as she buried her face against Katie's warm scalp and inhaled her daughter's baby-sweet fragrance.

But it was the clean, male scent of Ben Jackson that lingered in the air and in her senses, reminding her of all the lonely days she'd coped by herself, all the lonely nights she'd twisted and tossed in her solitary bed as she listened to the soft baby-snuffles-and-snores of Katie and Will.

Maybe that was why she'd seen the matching loneliness in Ben Jackson's face. From the cave where he'd buried it, his loneliness had called to hers, the melancholy notes slipping along her nerve ends and merging with the slow beat of her heart.

"Bathroom's behind this door, Will." Jackson pointed to a closed, scarred door with a bottom edge two inches from the floor.

Will didn't move.

Obviously puzzled by the boy's refusal to go to the bathroom since he'd been so urgent earlier, Ben didn't say anything, merely waited, giving her son time to make up his mind whether he wanted to leave the safety of his mother's side. Then, casually, as if an afterthought, Ben opened the warped bathroom door, pulled the light chain and said, "Let me check. We have a thumbnail-sized tree frog that likes to keep us company in here. Not knowing you, he might be scared. I'd sure hate to see him take off. He's a friendly little beast."

Will's expression was dubious, but Annie saw the sharpened interest in his quick glance at the man and his movement toward the bathroom.

Coming out of the bathroom, Ben Jackson said, "All clear. Take your time." Not appearing to pay any attention to Will's slow approach to the room, Jackson added, "We'll wait for you. I want to check out one of the shipments in here while I have the chance."

His fiction had been more elaborate than it needed to be, Annie thought as he crossed his arms and leaned patiently against the wall, waiting with her for Will to come out of the bathroom. But Will had needed that graceful, face-saving story.

"Will's a slowpoke," Katie offered from the comfort of Annie's arms.

"Yeah?"

As Katie nodded and nestled closer to Annie, they yawned at the same time, mouths cracking wide, Katie's eyes scrunching shut, and Annie laughed.

Listening to the silvery laugh, Ben wondered if sounds had colors in them. Her laugh was bright and gleaming, threaded with gold and red, its warmth sneaking into him and making him feel like a beggar at a stranger's hearth, making him crave more, making him want for that moment to be enclosed in the bright circle promised by her laugh.

He still didn't know why he'd turned back halfway to Azalea Park. He'd looked over at Annie Conroy sleeping with her children wrapped in her slim arms and remembered the car trunk filled with their belongings.

Remembered the crumpled box with red bows in it and whipped the truck around so fast the tires had squealed and she'd woken up.

Gabe was going to rag his ears off in the morning.

The door opened and Will came out, wiping his hands on his T-shirt. "I saw the tree frog. He's under the sink. I was very careful." He added earnestly, "I did not frighten him, Mr. Jackson."

Staring into Will's anxious eyes, Ben stooped and said, equally earnest, "I didn't think you would. I could tell you're a careful kind of guy." Ben nodded approvingly. "I like that in a man."

"You do?" Will tipped his head. "But I'm only *almost* a man. Maybe next year I will be all the way a man."

"Yeah. Wouldn't surprise me." Ben stood up. Will's apprehension made him want to avoid adding to the kid's long list of seemingly endless anxieties.

A kid that age should be thinking about kid stuff, not acting like a neurotic miniature adult. In spite of that miracle of a laugh, Annie Conroy wasn't doing such a red-hot job with her kids. Will jumped at shadows, and Katie wouldn't leave her side. He scowled in her direction.

Her stunned, slow blink, the droop of her gold-tipped eyelashes against her drawn paleness annoyed him.

Annoyed him, ticked him off and held him motionless, watching the lift of those eyelashes, the hurt in her eyes.

Hell. She'd caught his unspoken criticism. He scowled again, wanting to yell at her, wanting to kiss the stunned hurt away. He was angry with himself, angry with her because—

Why?

Gabe had been right. He was like a grizzly bear with its paw in a trap.

"Come on. I'll show you where you can sleep."

"Okay." Her voice was so low he almost missed her answer, and she shifted her daughter again, waiting for him to lead the way.

A shine of tears glazed the blue of her eyes.

Two feet below Ben's chin, Will glared at him.

Even Katie, from the perch in Annie Conroy's arms, regarded Ben reproachfully.

The kids had read the undercurrents between him and their mother with radarlike accuracy.

"What?" he snarled from the edge of the circle they'd drawn against him.

Will jumped, and Ben's blood pressure shot up.

"What?" he snarled again.

"Okay," Annie snapped right back. "I said 'okay.' Show us where you want us to go and we'll clear out of your way." She'd straightened and banished the tear-shine. Her mouth was pursed, its fullness becoming one pink softness.

"Up these stairs." Ben tucked his hands into his pockets. No matter what he did, he made things worse. Well, hell. He'd always known he wasn't any good around kids.

Around families.

He definitely wasn't a family man, he thought grimly, stalking up the stairs, Annie and her small family trailing woefully behind him.

Gesturing to the closed bedroom door down the hall, Ben said brusquely, "Gabe's gone to bed. Keep the noise down."

"Oh, we'll be quiet as mice. Or tree frogs." She smiled and fluttered her spiky eyelashes at him as Will snickered. "And we won't walk off with your towels. Or silver."

Annie Conroy had obviously recovered.

"Good." Anger washed from him with her cheekiness. He'd reacted, and badly, to the kids' anxiety, not meaning to hurt her.

But he had, and guilt had made him angry with himself, with her, and he'd lashed out.

He'd never reacted like that before.

Knowing he had a bred-in-the-bones nasty streak, he'd always backed off any time he started to care about something or someone, stayed away from involvement, stayed away from situations that could strip the reins out of his control.

Without control, he would become the very thing he'd worked all his life to destroy.

Judging from his behavior tonight, he couldn't escape himself. Well, his reaction to Annie and her children proved what he'd always suspected.

Emotions were dangerous.

Control was important.

Despite her fragile appearance, though, Annie Conroy hadn't lain down like a rug and let him walk all over her. She was a survivor.

Pushing open the door to the extra room, he said, "It has a bed, and that's about all. It's clean."

He'd kept the room empty of clutter. He didn't like possessions hanging around his neck, weighing him down. Remembering Annie's trunk filled with possessions, he thought the room looked barren. "Not much in here. I'll find whatever you and the kids need for the night. Let me know."

She scoped out the closet-size room, the double bed with its faded comforter, the uncurtained windows and the table below it. "An extra pillow, please, if it's not too much trouble." Again, the flutter of her gold-brushed eyelashes, the toss of her heavy hair with its elusive fragrance.

An army with her energy and sass could conquer the world. "No trouble. The three of you can sleep together in the bed?"

"Sure. We have before." She bit her lip. "Only once or twice," she amended too swiftly.

"Yeah?"

"On visits. Home. Holidays. With relatives and friends. You know."

He didn't. But he knew she was lying.

Her smile was too bright, too wide.

And Will, that child-barometer of the emotional atmosphere, dropped his eyes to the floor.

"Swell. There should be no problem, then."

"Absolutely none." Her smile never wavered. "One pillow is all we'll need from you. We've caused you enough trouble."

Not wasting energy denying the obvious, Ben tapped his fingertips against the door. "There's a bathroom down the hall, next to Gabe's room. It's frog-free," he noted for Will's benefit. "I'll leave a light on."

Pulling the door shut behind him, Ben heard the careful thump of shoes on the floor, the squeak of bedsprings squelched by Will's murmured, "Shh, Katie. You heard *him*. He'll kick us out, Katie, if you don't watch it."

Ben had never expected to be a *him*.

He didn't think he liked it, either.

"Listen, puddin'-heads, Mr. Jackson has been extraordinarily helpful. We've intruded on his home, and he's helped us. We owe him."

The bedsprings squeaked once more as Ben walked away.

Searching all over for an extra pillow, he finally grabbed the one from his own bed and put a clean pillowcase on it.

Pillow in hand, he tapped lightly on the door.

Annie opened the door but kept it as a barrier between them.

Through the gap, Ben saw Katie and Will lying flat under the sheet and striped comforter. They'd drawn the sheet up to their noses and two sets of blue eyes, one light, one dark, observed him silently.

"Thanks." Her wrist brushed the palm of his hand as she grasped the pillow, tugging at it.

His focus on Will and Katie, Ben didn't release the pillow. It was the graze of Annie's skin against his that had his concentration swinging fully to her.

And then he understood why she was staying half-hidden behind the door. She'd changed, and the bit of dark green fabric dipping and slithering over her delicate curves almost managed to reach the top of her thighs.

Through the cut-out sleeves as she carefully extended her hand, Ben still glimpsed one smooth breast.

He didn't intend to let his knuckle brush against that flower-softness, but she tugged and the pillow was still in his hand, and he couldn't help it, he really couldn't, but his knuckle shivered against the rosy nub.

At the stroke of his knuckle, the tip peaked.

Ben dropped the pillow.

Annie clutched it to her.

Clenching his pillow in front of her so tightly that it looked as if she were wearing it, she took a shallow breath, and her barely heard gasp slammed right down to the center of his being.

He wanted to look away from her, but he couldn't. His whole world narrowed until the only thing in it was Annie Conroy with her dazed eyes, her trembling mouth and her pale pink softness.

He stepped forward.

She stepped back, shutting the door as his hand reached out.

Unable to move, Ben remained with his hand flat against the door, sweat beading his forehead. Pulsing hard and painfully, a primitive urge rose and tightened, urging him to break down the bedroom door, that primal urge a fierce thrumming deep in his blood.

When he could finally move, his hands were shaking and he still felt the tender heat of her nipple against his knuckle. Rubbing his bent finger against his mouth again and again, scrubbing away at that heat, Ben thought he tasted the sweetness of her skin on his lips with each hard scrub.

Annie Conroy was trouble, all right.

Lying awake in his bed down the hall, his bedroom door shut, hers tightly closed, Ben believed he could hear her cheek brush against her sheets, believed he could hear her breathing softly into the clean pillowcase of his pillow, believed he heard the beating of her heart drumming hard, calling him.

Against his own sheets, his bare skin burned and burned and he dreamed before morning that he touched Annie Conroy's flushed skin, traced its shimmering heat to her beating core.

He awoke the next morning to knotted sheets and an aching that both filled him *and* left him desolate.

Christmas was two days away and Santa Claus nowhere in sight.

Sitting on the edge of his bed, holding his head in his hands, Ben heard for real the subdued giggle as shoes brushed by his door and continued to the bathroom.

A bright winter sun splashed the floor in front of him.

He couldn't hide forever behind his closed door.

He wanted to, though.

As he yanked on an ironed pair of Levis, he heard another pair of feet traipse past his door. Jamming his arms through the sleeves of a shirt, he thought about his behavior, the dilemma he'd created for himself.

Slowly buttoning up his white shirt, he considered what had to be done. He had to inform Gabe they had visitors, although Gabe had probably figured that out for himself by now. He tucked the tails of his shirt into the jeans and zipped. Annie's car had to be repaired.

He could still drive her to Azalea Park today, but he knew with an absolute certainty that he wouldn't be able to find anybody to work on her car, not this close to Christmas.

If they were closer to Bradenton or Venice, there would be no problem, but Azalea Park was as sleepy and slow-moving as any town fifty years ago. Time hadn't slowed in Azalea, it had run down to a full stop.

Until now, he'd considered that drowsy pace a plus.

He dragged on boots, thunking his heels hard on the floor. Hell, everybody was up and moving except him.

He'd locked himself into a trick box, and the magician hadn't left the instructions for escaping.

And Gabe sure wouldn't be any help, Ben thought as he went downstairs to the bar and saw Gabe ambling over to Annie and her kids with a plate filled with scrambled eggs and a tray filled with coffee cups and mugs of milk.

Sheesh. Gabe knew better than to put milk in the beer mugs.

At least he had until Annie Conroy had waltzed into his bar with her vulnerable wide-eyed helplessness that hid that grit in her character. Under the spell of her and her children, Gabe would be absolutely useless in speeding her on her way and out of their lives. Some partner, Gabe was.

Startled by the whack of boots on the bare floor, the breakfast club looked up at him, all four heads turning in synchronization. He was the party-crasher, their chumminess abracadabraing him into an outsider in his own bar.

"Mornin', old son." Gabe shoved a chair in Ben's direction. "Pull up a chair and grab a bite."

After his restless night, Ben felt like taking a bite out of somebody's hide. "I've got chores waiting for me."

"That so?" Gabe tipped the chair back and forth. "Too busy to set a spell and catch up on the latest news?"

"News?" Tipping his straw, cowboy-style hat down over his eyes, Ben folded his arms and waited. Not going to be a good day, not by a long shot.

The sly humor in Gabe's narrowed eyes set Ben's teeth on edge. The old coot had something up his sleeve, and if past history were any guideline, Ben knew he was going to come out with the short end of the stick.

"Sure. I hired us a waitress to see us through the holidays." To give Gabe his due, he did seem to be struggling to get through his announcement with a straight face, and his sheepish grin was worth a dollar or two.

"Did you now?" Ben leaned against the wall and crossed his boots at the ankle. "Thought we didn't need any help. Thought this was a slow time of the year." He thumped his boot toes together in time to the ticking of the clock over the bar and waited for Gabe to dig his way out of the hole he'd fallen into.

"Like the man said, 'The times they are a-changin'.' Got to keep up with the times, or the whole wide world'll pass us by, old son." Gabe was working on his sincere look, his shrewd blue eyes projecting candor with everything he had to give.

Like he'd figured last night. Death and taxes and Annie Conroy in his life. Some things were inevitable, but he didn't have to make life easy for the four musketeers. "Don't know as I want to keep the bar open over Christmas this year." He tapped his toes together and studied the floor. "No sense fighting the tide, I reckon. Everybody else closes up around here. I decided to go with the flow, be a mellow fellow, chill out, as the man says." Ben figured *some* man must have said one of those.

Choking, Gabe spewed coffee onto the floor. "Damned if you did!"

"Damned if I didn't," Ben drawled, watching the sun gild Annie Conroy's hair. In his dreams during the night, her hair had been shining like that, like heavy satin rippling with light. "So we won't be needing any extra help, even if we were expecting a horde of tourists back here in the piney woods."

He straightened and strolled over to the table. "More coffee, anybody?"

There were smudged shadows under Annie Conroy's eyes and he wondered if she'd dreamed, too.

Her subdued "That's okay, Mr. Thibideaux" was meant for Gabe, but Ben heard it.

"I think me and my partner need to have a conference if y'all will excuse us for one short minute. Or five." Shooting Ben an evil glower and snagging his partner's shirt sleeve, Gabe turned and graced Annie of the Shining Hair and her children with his courtliest half bow. "Y'all stay right where you are while I straighten out a thing or two." Gabe's skinny chest actually swelled up with self-importance. "I'm the senior partner in this establishment."

Putting up a token resistance, Ben let Gabe drag him behind the bar.

"Ben, you got to stop this fooling around. That angel and her children got kicked out of her apartment up in Chicago. She came down here expecting to stay a while with her grandma, but the old lady wound up falling and busting her hip, so she's in a nursing home. Who knows when she'll get out, but in the meantime, Annie and the kids got no place to go, a busted car and about enough money to fix the car *if* they're lucky and it's something I can fix for 'em. We got to help 'em, Ben. It's Christmas. I hired her for a week or two, to let her get on her feet. Even *you* wouldn't turn 'em away now, would you, Ben?"

Looking over, Ben caught Will's steady stare. The kid knew Gabe didn't have the final word, knew their fate rested in Ben's hands.

Feeling the walls closing in, trapping him, Ben smashed the crown of his hat down flat and said, meaning every one of his quietly uttered words, "Damn you, Gabe."

Annie's skirt fluttered at the edge of his vision as he slammed out the back door.

Chapter Four

Annie followed on Ben Jackson's heels, out the door and down the back path to the shed. The small building leaned haphazardly at the border of cleared ground and scrubland filled with cabbage palms and wire grass dotted with sandy hillocks of vegetation.

She didn't know what to expect.

She would never have expected to see him in his white shirt mucking out the ground around a glossy-skinned black horse contentedly munching oats from a feed bunk.

Though she'd teased him about camping out in a stable, she hadn't seen him as a man who would enjoy stable work. She should have realized that he hadn't gotten his muscled body doing nothing more than tending bar.

But then she hadn't been thinking clearly about a number of things last night—even *before* her car died along the road. Her decisions for several weeks had been shaped by a downward spiraling series of events and she'd been caught in the tornadolike effect as everything blew away, leaving her stranded on a back road in Florida.

He ignored her as she stepped into the cool shade of the shed, working steadily at the straw and ordure on the ground as he cleared his way through one side and worked toward where she stood at the entrance.

Waiting for him to decide whether or not he was going to talk to her, Annie planned to give him about three more passes through the muck before she took matters into her own hands.

Even in the relative coolness of the shed on a December day, he'd already worked up a sweat. A wet, dark line ran down the center of his back and pasted the white cotton to his spine. With each thrust and heave of the heavy pitchfork, the dark line widened, outlining the ridges of muscle transversing his shoulders and ribs.

Casting her an enigmatic glance from under the brim of his light-colored straw hat, he continued the ferocity of his attack.

That did it. He'd had his chance. "Mr. Jackson—"

He jabbed the tines into a stack of hay. "You might as well call me Ben." Unfolding in one smooth move, he tossed the hay to one side. "So what do you want, *Annie?*" Stopping, he jammed the pitchfork into the ground, and, like a tuning fork, it vibrated to his mood.

"Well, *Ben,* your partner offered me a job." Watching where she placed her black leather flats, Annie took two tentative steps into the shed.

"Yeah. I heard. I was there, remember?" He cocked his head and ran one hand down the side of his neck, flicking sweat away. "That about it, Annie? Because I'd like to get back to work if that's all you have to say."

A dusty smell of grass and horse mingled with a faint, clean tang that Annie recognized as his own male smell, vital and earthy.

With a forefinger, he pushed his hat to the back of his head. Sweat mixed with bits of straw still glistened on his forehead and neck. Coming through an open square in the roof, a shaft of sunlight filtered through dust motes and gently circling straw flecks to gleam on the toe of one well-oiled leather boot poking through a clot of hay and straw.

Even mucking out a shed, Ben Jackson wore polished boots. Annie couldn't decide if she found that detail funny or somehow sad.

He was a man indifferent to kids, but who somehow understood her son's trepidations and addressed them without making a big deal out of Will's fears. He looked at her with hunger, but with each antagonistic word, each push-away action, he warned her to keep her distance.

But then he'd touched her, reluctantly, deliberately, and she'd burned with that feathery touch all night long.

She'd never known anyone who turned her expectations upside down the way he did.

"Come on, Annie. Speak your piece unless you've only come out here to admire the scenery." He twisted his mouth into a smile and watched her with those cat eyes. "Lots of folks come to Florida for the scenery." A dark teasing in the way he leaned against the pitchfork, his powerful arm raised to grasp the long handle and his muscles defined by the stance, his lean hips angled casually, but nothing at all relaxed or friendly in the tightly controlled lines of his face. "Is that why you're out here? For the scenery?" His voice dipped low and velvety. "You a tourist, Ms. Conroy?"

"No." She'd botched it. She should have planned what she wanted to say, not rushed after him.

"You look like a tourist, all dressed up in your best blue blouse and ready to go touring."

Not knowing how to approach him in this mood, she abandoned pride in the clear, revealing light of day and chose blunt truth. "I *need* the job Gabe offered me."

He released his grasp on the pitchfork and straightened, his expression shutting her out as she tried to continue.

"Gabe said—" She cleared her throat. "He suggested—"

Each word was an effort, cutting to her soul.

She didn't want to beg for this job.

But she would.

Pride was a luxury she could no longer afford. For some reason, last night she'd thought she could still untangle the mess her life had become in the last few weeks.

If there were a loose end to the knotted strand of her problems, she couldn't find it.

She'd reached that terrifying truth while she lay sleepless during the night, burning with the touch of Ben Jackson.

"I don't know whether Gabe made his offer out of charity or whether you really need a waitress, but I don't care." Forgetting to watch her step in her need to convince him, she walked over to him and touched his arm. The straw along the damp, hot skin of his muscled forearm scratched her finger. "Please."

"It wasn't charity." His voice was rusty, as if he hadn't talked in days, harsh, and she didn't care if he was telling her the truth or not.

"Two weeks. Three." She gripped his arm, trying to make him see how much she needed this job. "At least until after New Year's."

Dust motes settled around her, on her eyelashes, and she blinked. "I'm begging—"

"You've got the job." He pivoted, his abrupt movement kicking up clouds of dirt and straw. "You can stay above the bar." He turned again, suddenly, and glared at her. "And don't you dare say thank-you in that prissy little tone you use, or you're fired." Seizing the pitchfork, he dug deeply into one particularly noisome pile. "Now go away and let me get back to work."

Shaken, Annie left the shed. Sagging against a pine tree, she tried to regain her composure before returning to Katie and Will. During the night, as Ben had driven them to her car and toward Azalea Park, she'd really believed she was acting rationally, sensibly.

If he'd left them in that town, she wouldn't have been able to find a job. And she would have used up her financial resources repairing her car.

Two weeks would have flown by. School would have been approaching...

She shuddered.

At least now she had a chance to rest, to think clearly and sort out what she had to do if she wasn't going to wind up on the street again.

Two weeks.

As she breathed in the fresh air tinged with a faraway scent of orange blossoms, she stretched out her arms to the warm sun. Two weeks! An eternity. She could do *anything* with two weeks.

And tomorrow was Christmas Eve.

Annie flew back to the bar. "Will! Katie! Come here, punkin. Guess what?"

Will met her halfway and she lifted him into her arms, swinging him in a delirious whirl up and down and around until she was dizzy and he was giggling and Katie was chasing them first one way and then the other until they all fell in a heap under an oak tree, laughing until her tears splattered onto Will and he made her swear she was laughing because Christmas was around the corner. She swore, crossing her heart, that she was laughing because she was so happy.

And she was, she was.

She was giddy with happiness.

By the time she'd recovered herself enough to give Katie her twirl, Gabe had shuffled out to join them.

"What did the boss say?"

"I thought *you* were the senior partner," she teased gently, wanting to throw her arms around his skinny shoulders.

"I am." He shrugged. "But Ben runs the place. I might have given you the wrong idea." His smile was devilish. "You staying, then?"

"Until New Year's."

"All right." He nodded with satisfaction. "That's good."

"You can't imagine how good," she breathed.

"Reckon I could." He studied her for a long moment. "We'll take a look at your car later today." As he left, his reedy voice, flat and wandering in and out of tempo, drifted back to her. "'O little town of Bethlehem . . .'"

As he shut the back door to the bar, she heard a mildly ribald line of "Jingle Bells," and giggled. She'd have to watch out or the sneaky old gentleman would have Katie lisping the rest of the verse.

"We're staying?" Will climbed onto her lap. He'd never been a demonstrative child, not even as a baby, and she cherished the moments when he allowed her to be "lovey-dovey," as he called it disdainfully. "For sure?"

"Yes, yes, and yes!" She hugged him once because he permitted it, and the second time because she needed to. Then she noogied his belly. He snorted, a polite, held-in snort, but genuine for all his restraint. "And Christmas is day after tomorrow, puddin'-head."

"But no p'sents," said Katie mournfully, leaning over and resting the sharp point of her elbow on Annie's shoulder.

"No, punkin. Not this year."

The wrapped presents had been in the apartment. She hadn't been able to salvage them.

Through the open door as they'd left, she'd seen the brilliant splash of colors under the tree and remembered the nights she'd stayed up late to wrap each one. Realizing she had to leave Katie and Will's Christmas behind, Annie thought she'd hit bottom.

"Don't be dopey, Katie," Will instructed. "We got big problems this year. Anyway, presents are for babies." He climbed off Annie's lap.

"I am a baby. I should have a p'sent." Katie worked her chin into Annie's neck.

"You're not a baby anymore, Katie," Will said, stalking back to the bar.

Tagging behind him, Katie asserted, "Santa Claus will find me."

"Lot you know." Will disappeared into the bar.

Annie wasn't even tempted to lie back under the tree. She had too much to do. Leaping to her feet, she ran after Katie and Will while ideas zigzagged through her brain.

Tipping the plastic water bottle to his lips, Ben let water trickle down his face and wash away the itchy sweat and straw.

His itch went deeper than water would wash away. Annie Conroy had hated asking him for the job. Her husky voice had eaten away at him until he'd surrendered to the inevitable.

No matter how much he wanted her out of his sight and his life, he hadn't been able to let her finish her awkward speech. Nobody should have to beg. Not for anything.

Water dripped down his shirtfront. It was going to be a long two weeks.

Seagull whuffled through his nose and moved sideways toward Ben, nudging his shoulder. Standing shadowed at the shed entrance, Ben watched Annie whirl Will in a swoop of skirt and color-blur, her face tipped to the sun, her laughing voice coming to him on the mild air and winding through him in a slow, painful current.

When she collapsed with Will and Katie into a giggling heap on the ground, her skirt fanned like a peacock's tail of greens and blues and pinks around her, settling in a fold of color back from one long thigh. The colors glowed against her Yankee-pale skin.

He thought for a moment she was crying. Stepping backward, deeper into the shed, he watched like a kid with his nose pressed against the toy-store window as she rocked Will against her, her love for her children shining in the pure oval of her face, shining to him in the dark shadows.

He stayed there until she ran to the back door behind Will and Katie, and pausing there, she looked toward the shed, shading her eyes with her hand as she lingered with one foot on the ground, one on the step.

As she lifted her hand, the cloudy blue sleeve of her shimmery blouse slid back, revealing the tender gleam of her underarm.

He wanted to trace that gleaming skin with his mouth, wanted to slide his lips all the way down to the edge of the slippery blue sleeve and beyond, beyond to her warm skin underneath, wanted to linger there, tasting, touching.

He wanted her.

That wasn't his problem. *Wanting* a woman had never been a problem.

He understood the craving of flesh. That was simple, a pleasurable dance of bodies meeting and separating.

What he didn't understand was his yearning for this woman. Not for *a* woman, any woman, but for *her*, for Annie Conroy.

Oh, it was very specific, this craving. Something more than that ancient dance of male and female.

Terrifying. And not simple at all.

The back door slammed shut. She was gone.

But the aching way down inside remained, a piercing need.

He'd reconciled himself to her presence for one day. Turning the grooming brushes over and over in his hands, Ben wondered how he was going to get through the next two weeks.

Stroking the brushes against Seagull's sleek hide, he thought of Annie's satiny hair slipping through his fingers.

He gave Seagull the grooming of the horse's life.

Ben stayed out in the shed all morning, cleaning. Cobwebs caught on his hat, grayed his shirt. Dirt and oil smeared his jeans in wide streaks he doubted he'd ever get out as he dug through barrels and crates jammed in a hodgepodge.

Over the years until Ben arrived and bought half of the bar and its surrounding land, Gabe had used the shed as a catchall. It had caught about all it could hold. For some time, Ben had been planning a major overhaul, working slowly to convince Gabe that things that hadn't seen the light of day in years weren't worth keeping.

Then, three weeks ago, Ben had bought Seagull. Gabe agreed that the shed had now become a high priority chore, but he said Ben would have to go through the stuff. Gabe didn't want to. Ben had never had a pet, never wanted one, and sure hadn't aimed on bringing an eight-hundred-pound, twenty-year-old horse into his life.

But Gabe had conned Ben into going to the estate auction of a farm near Okeechobee City. Everything on the ranch had to be sold. The horse came up for sale toward the end of the day, and by then most of the bidders had left. Dusty and shaggy with neglect, the horse had three strikes against it. No one had wanted the ancient gelding.

Ben hadn't wanted it, either.

Seagull nudged Ben's rear end. Absentmindedly, Ben scratched the horse's nose and surveyed the pile of boxes remaining.

Gabe, unlike Ben, liked to hold on to his *stuff*. And Gabe had a lot of *stuff*, Ben acknowledged, dragging out one more moldy box. "Damned old coot," he swore as the box disintegrated onto the ground, spilling a stack of fly-spotted magazines and newspapers in front of him. "Hell." He squatted and thumbed through the stacks. Magazines, envelopes with faded and illegible addresses, the front page of a November 23, 1963, *Tampa Tribune,* all crumbled between his fingers.

Ben had been two years old, Gabe forty-three, the same age as Ben's father.

All these papers the old man had considered important, now crumbling and disintegrating. Stuff, just stuff Gabe had collected. His past.

Ben stood, scrubbing his hands clean of flecks of newsprint and dirt.

Who needed reminders of the past, anyway?

Rotating the spigot, Ben turned on the water to the hose and let it run free for a few seconds. He gulped from the stream as he directed it toward the water trough. Whinnying, Seagull drank with him.

"Move over, you selfish, knock-kneed, glue-factory reject." Ben hip-bumped Seagull to one side. "Come on, you old slug. Quit hogging the water." Holding the hose and off balance, he bumped the horse again.

Unexpectedly, Seagull pushed his wet muzzle hard against Ben's chest, thumping Ben to the floor where he sat flat on his rear looking straight into the distressed eyes of Annie Conroy's son.

"Is the horse mad at you?"

Ben said, "Nope. He's joking with me."

"Horses don't joke."

"Could have fooled me," Ben muttered, throwing Seagull a scowl.

"Are you mad at him?"

Jeez Louise. The kid would worry himself into an early grave at this rate. Or maybe all kids were worrywarts. "I'm not mad at Seagull."

Will held out his hand. "Want me to help you up? I helped Gramma out of her chair."

"No thanks, I can get up, but I think I'll stay right where I am." So the kid thought he was a *him*, and as old as Gramma. Good thing Ben's ego was in halfway decent shape. It was a wonder anybody decided to have kids.

But Annie and her kids were a matched set. She always seemed to be touching them as if they were as much a part of her as her own skin. Ben couldn't imagine her without them, a constant in her life.

Personally, he preferred freedom, variety. Anything constant became a chain sooner or later. Motioning to the ground, Ben said, "Have a seat."

Considering the shed's floor with the same fastidious examination his mother had given it, Will said dubiously, "Here?"

Then Annie had forgotten the condition of the ground and walked over to him, begging him in a strained, carefully controlled voice for a nothing job. Ben drew a deep breath past the constriction in his chest.

"Hey, Seagull's telling me to take a time-out. I can take a hint. Want some water?" Ben held out the hose to him.

Will shook his head. "No. Not thirsty." Storklike, he stood on one foot, the other angled in back of him. "Thank you."

Sighing, Ben got to his feet. He twisted the spigot handle to the "off" position. Water dripped into the dirt as he rolled the hose back onto the hook on the shed wall. Damned if today wasn't turning out to be Conference with the Conroys Day. Maybe he should post a sign-up sheet for them.

"Mr. Gabe told me to say lunch was ready and you should haul your rear end inside if you don't want to be left out," he recited in a rush.

"That sounds like Gabe, all right." Ben levered himself onto a low shelf bolted along the wall. "I'm not hungry."

"You didn't eat breakfast." Will now balanced on his other leg. "You might get sick. You could get a cold and then pneumonia." He wrapped his arms around himself as he balanced. "I read that in a book. It's possible."

"True." Scraping one boot heel against the edge of the shelf, Ben wondered what Will had in mind. "But missing a meal or two isn't likely to make me sick. I'll survive."

"That's what Mommy says. 'We'll survive, Will. Don't worry.' She says that all the time. Especially now."

"Yeah?" Ducking his head, Ben scraped his other heel and instep slowly against the shelf edge.

Will nodded. "But I worry."

Ben checked the bottom of his boots, one after the other. "Lot for a guy to think about, I reckon."

"Oh, boy." Will's shoulders winged up around his ears. "All the time. And I think this time we *are* in the soup." He lowered his arms and leg and squared his hunched shoulders. "I know how to weed."

"Excuse me?"

"I weeded in Chicago. For Skeeter. We traded," Will explained. "Skeeter fixed our car, and I weeded his yard. He said it was a fair trade."

Rubbing his chin, Ben frowned. "You're offering to weed?"

Will nodded. "A fair trade. For letting us stay here. For giving Mommy a job."

Looking at Will's thin face, Ben saw Annie's determination reflected there. "Gabe hired your mom. You don't owe me anything." Ben's voice was gruff.

"Maybe not." Studying him, Will said, "Maybe we do. Mr. Gabe said you have final say-so." He stumbled on the phrase.

"Not always. This was Gabe's decision, kid."

"Maybe." Doubt showed in every inch of Will's body, and then he nodded. "I will pick up and weed in front. Fair trade, okay?" Will trotted over and stuck out his hand at Ben.

"Okay," Ben said, shaking the boy's hand. If picking up bottles and paper around the bar stopped the kid from worrying about things, it *would* be a fair trade.

"You coming in for lunch?"

"Nope." Swinging his legs to the ground, Ben stood up.

"You're mad at Mr. Gabe."

"Yeah, that I am."

"Because of us." Will headed to the door. "I told Mommy we shouldn't stay, but she said I was worrying too much again. I knew you didn't want us here."

Before Ben could stop him, Will was a thin profile in the entrance of the shed, blocking the light, and then the sun streamed in once more as Ben stared at the empty frame of the entrance through a haze of rising and falling dust motes.

Later, sticky with grime and the residue from Gabe's *stuff*, Ben cat-walked through the back of the bar and headed upstairs, bypassing Gabe's tea party with the Conroys.

Silently taking the stairs two at a time, he paused at the round panel of stained glass set midway in the wall of the stairway. From the bar side, the stained glass was a picture of bears in a rushing creek. From the staircase side, the stained glass showed him Annie sitting at the bar with Gabe. The glimpse of her black leather shoe perched at the end of her vigorously seesawing leg halted him midstep.

Elbows plopped on the bar, she leaned forward, her long legs dangling and swinging back and forth from the bar stool. The sweet oval of her face was close to Gabe's wrinkled one, and she kept shoving a heavy swath of brown-gold hair back from her face as they talked.

Lingering, Ben watched her, caught by her face glowing with animation. Last night she'd been drawn with fatigue, but today she was in constant motion, the smudges under her eyes the only evidence of her ordeal. Dancing her slim fingers across the top of the bar, she tilted her head first one way, then the other as she wrinkled her nose. Two enormous gold stars swung from the shell of each ear and tinkled gently as she moved.

And the whole time, he stood watching. She swiveled the bar stool back and forth, the round curve of each hip swinging first toward him and then away. With each swing, her blouse pulled at the waist, tightening against her breasts and clinging to the small bumps of her nipples under the silky blue.

The voices floated up the stairs after him no matter how fast he moved through the hall.

"Are Katie and Will going to be in the way, Gabe?" Anxiety poked through Annie's cheerfulness.

"We'll keep 'em out of the bar when it's open. Some legal mumbo jumbo. We won't worry about it, okay, angel?"

Will's giggle was the last sound Ben heard as he quietly closed the bathroom door, turned the shower on full blast and stepped under the stinging hot spray, letting it drum against his scalp in a futile effort to wash away his self-disgust and his memories.

Too many memories mingling with the water streaming against his face. Too many to wash away even if he stayed forever under the inadequate baptism of his shower.

Gabe wanted to hold on to his past, all its moldering detritus.

Turning his face up to the pounding spray, Ben wished his past would swirl down the drain as easily as the pieces of straw that circled and circled before swooshing down into darkness with the cleansing burst of the cooling spray.

Nothing would cleanse him.

No matter how much he wanted to deny the past, he was what he was. What his history had made him.

He could clean out Gabe's shed in a day, destroying the old man's trash, but he couldn't destroy the trash in his own life that easily.

There was no escape for him.

He'd never expected one.

Buttoning the cuffs of a white shirt, Ben walked downstairs. He flattened his wet hair against his skull, flicking drops of water away, and entered the bar. As Gabe, Annie and her kids looked up at him, just as they had at breakfast, he again felt like the odd man out.

Something in his expression drew Annie off the stool and toward him. In her haste, she trapped the low heel of her shoe on the rung of the stool. Tipping forward, she tried to balance herself by clutching at the slippery bar surface.

Reaching her side in one long stride, Ben tangled with the hem of her striped skirt caught on the round seat, and under that concealing curtain, his palms slid over silky skin and stopped at a lacy edge as her chin bumped his nose, and hung up between stool and him, she laughed.

"Oops." She wiggled her foot free of her shoe as he held her to him, her feet off the floor, his palms cupping her to him. "We've got to stop meeting this way."

Her hair swung into his face, clinging to his jaw, momentarily blinding him in its sweet fragrance and he inhaled, his thumbs slipping forward against that enticing lace.

And as she swung her hair free, her face went furiously red with awareness.

He let her slide down, his hands closing around her waist and steadying her until she could stand.

Blotchy red remained on her cheeks as she rushed into speech, moving toward the bar, toward the door, toward the stool, a carousel of color with her skirt whipping around her. "I'm not usually this clumsy. Truly. You'll never trust me with a tray of food and drinks after this, but, really, I swear, I'm not accident-prone. Not ordinarily. Not usually." Her eyes looked everywhere except at him, and her words came in staccato, gasping bursts.

And with his arms empty at his side, Ben knew he'd had heaven in his grasp and had turned it loose.

Chapter Five

Clasping her hands tightly together, Annie stared through the windshield of the truck. The late-afternoon sun shone in on Ben's side, making it difficult for her to see his expression. He hadn't spoken to her since the moment she'd tumbled into his arms off the bar stool.

Of course, to be perfectly fair to the surly beast, she hadn't said anything to *him* either. She hadn't known what to say, but surely a twenty-six-year-old divorced woman ought to be able to handle life in the nineties with a bit more panache than she'd shown with Ben Jackson.

Maybe she could have, but she hadn't had a whole lot of *eighties* experience to build on, either. She'd fallen right through the cracks of the sexual revolution.

Marrying two days after high school graduation and having Will within the year had turned her into an adult overnight.

Annie rubbed her skirt over her knee and gripped her hands together again. She had to stop fidgeting.

Marriage with Larry hadn't prepared her for men like Ben Jackson.

Ben was way beyond her pitiful experience.

Lighthearted, playful, will-of-the-wisp Larry had been another child for her to bring up except, unlike Will and Katie, Larry didn't change. He'd never grown past a cheerful teenage irresponsibility.

She'd thought he *might* change, might eventually accept the reality of bills and kids and adult life.

After all, she had.

Someone had to take care of the three of them, and, eventually, the four of them after Katie poked her nose into the world, a wide-eyed, unplanned sweetheart who'd made Annie realize that she was never going to be able to depend on Larry.

And somewhere during those five years, her love for that teenage boy who'd charmed her into loving him disappeared, buried under the weight of unending responsibility.

She'd really understood that clearly one night as she wiped down the kitchen table after he'd left the last of the children's milk out, souring it. She'd filed for a separation the next day during her lunch hour.

Somebody always had to pay the bills, deal with dirty diapers and take out the trash. Until their divorce, she'd always been the *someone*.

Not that the divorce had changed that. She was still cleaning up after Larry.

If she'd ever had worries that she'd given up on him too soon, this last incident—coming right after Thanksgiving—had swept any of those doubts cleanly out the door. It had also swept away the last of her savings.

She hadn't been softheaded enough to keep rescuing him after everything she'd been through. But this time she'd been *forced* to pay off debts he'd run up in her name. Larry had kept one of the credit cards and lied to her about canceling it, changing the address with the company so that she'd never gotten any bills, never known about owing a sum of money so large that she still couldn't think about it without hyperventilating.

In his phone call to tell her that she could expect some problems, he had been funny, joking and expecting her to find the humor in what was for her a complete and final disaster. Larry had never been able to see that life was a web of interconnecting responsibilities with people depending on you not to let them down at every point in the web.

Leaving her to work out the legal details and settle up, he'd vanished into the sunset.

At one point during the divorce, she'd tried to hate him, desperately needing a clean, antiseptic ending to their relationship, but she'd been unable to hate the man-boy who'd given her the two greatest gifts in her life, Will and Katie.

During the first years of their marriage, thinking love demanded total sacrifice, she'd forgiven him and forgiven him, might have kept repeating that destructive pattern if his irresponsibility hadn't involved Katie and Will.

She still couldn't forgive him for that failure.

Now she had to draw on her inadequate experience in order to deal with an embarrassingly awkward moment with this man who'd probably been born knowing everything about women.

It was in the way he walked.

That easy, smooth movement of his body made her think of slow-dancing and other things that a responsible, divorced mother with two dependents didn't have time to *think* about, much less *do* anything about, Annie decided in a righteous flurry of indignation, resenting the way her body softened every time he touched her, brushed against her, looked at her.

Not ordinarily a person who enjoyed confrontations, Annie decided that the situation needed addressing. The next two weeks would be impossible if that crackling between her and Ben Jackson wasn't discussed. She was actually proud of herself for not burying the moment somewhere deep in her subconscious and pretending it had never happened, pretending that it wouldn't happen again.

It would.

Even in her inexperience, that much was obvious to her.

Like lava pushing slowly down the mountainside, the sizzle crackling between them would burn and destroy everything in its way.

If she didn't resolve the situation, she wouldn't be able to work at the Star. They would run out of glasses and plates in two days. And heaven help anyone who came near her while she had a knife in her hand.

Pulling her knees up under her skirt, Annie gripped them as tightly as she could in order to still her inner shaking as she decided to plunge into forbidding waters. "Look, Ben, what happened back there was an accident. I know that."

"Was it?" His wrists rested lightly against the steering wheel of the truck, one thumb moving against the plastic in time to some music only he could hear.

That stroke of his rough thumb against her bare hip had made her tremble uncontrollably, that trembling rolling through her like the downward sweep on an amusement park roller-coaster ride, her stomach plummeting and quivering until she'd been unable to stand, think, or talk.

"Of course it was. You didn't mean to—" So much for nineties panache. She couldn't even put into words what he'd done.

"I didn't? Are you sure?" he drawled, sending one eyebrow up.

"Absolutely. It was an accident, a slip—"

"Like that silky one that bunched up in my hands?"

"Not—" She couldn't finish, heat flowing through her slow and sweet as she remembered how her slip had slithered through his fingers over her thigh. "Um—"

"Or maybe what happened was like a Freudian slip on my part? You know how it goes. There's no such thing as an *accident?* So Freud would tell you that maybe, way down in my subconscious I really chose to touch you, chose to feel you slide against me like cream into coffee.''

Annie couldn't think straight, didn't know how to handle him in this strange mood, didn't know how to stop his politely conversational flow of teasing words that turned her into Jell-O, quivering and vibrating to each unruffled comment he made in his low-pitched voice. "Okay, I'm trying to clarify the situation between us. I don't go around tripping and falling into men's arms. I don't have time for games like that. I thought what happened was an accident—that's what *I'd* rather think—I don't know what *you* wanted. Whatever happened, though, it's over and done with now.''

He shifted in his seat, and the seat belt twisted across his chest. Straightening the nylon edges, he said, "Come on, Annie, don't disappoint me. I'm waiting for you to say it won't happen again. If you can convince me that you didn't feel anything here—'' he touched her just below her left breast and her skin fluttered "—I might believe that we're only talking about an accidental bump-and-run.'' He smiled, a gently derisive lift of his lips.

"You know I can't say that,'' she whispered through dry lips, her heart banging against the spot he'd touched. She'd been right. Ben Jackson was definitely out of her league.

"Ah. An honest woman. But I expected that from you, Annie Conroy. I really did.'' Without taking his eyes off the road, he reached over to her hands chaining her to her knees. His broad palm enclosing hers, he pried her hands free, finger by locked finger. "You can relax now. You've made everything perfectly clear to me. We'll pretend that my touching you, my caveman urge to haul you upstairs as fast as I could so that I could have my wicked way with you, was nothing more than an accident. We'll pretend the pounding in my blood had nothing to do with the way you felt leaning against me, nothing at all to do with my craving to see if your skin tastes as delicious as it looks." He worked his fingers between hers until his wrist rested on her wrist, and she felt his pulse beat to the frantic beat of hers. "I understand, Annie. It was only an accident."

Keeping his long fingers folded around hers, he glanced at her, all the mockery absent from his intense eyes. "But who're you kidding, Annie? Yourself, maybe? Because I know what's happening between us." He shook their clasped hands. "I can feel your pulse thrumming like a wild thing in my hand. Did you know that, Annie?"

Helpless, she nodded. His pulse was racing so fast against her wrist while his voice was cool, composed, removed from that slam-bamming rhythm passing from him to her and back again until she couldn't breathe.

"Did you know you flush right here every time I *accidentally* touch you?" He lifted their joined hands and ran them down the side of her neck to the neckline of her blouse, tracing the semicircle above her breasts while her skin burned and shivered to the slow movement of their joined hands. "Is that rush of pink an *accident*, too?"

He released her hand and she clenched it in the folds of her skirt.

"I thought we needed to talk—" Her nerves were twanging against the prison of her skin. Pressed against the vinyl of the truck seat, the backs of her thighs heated, tingled with the pulsing blood rushing through her body as his words created dark, secret images behind her closed eyelids, images that she couldn't endure.

She opened her eyes.

Sunset-red bathed his hands and cast the fleeting shadows of roadside trees across his face. "I *know* what I need." The planes of his face seemed sharper in the twilight reds and purples. "And talking isn't about to satisfy me. But if you're interested in anything besides talking, let me know, okay?"

"No, no. I'm not." She shook her head violently, trying to shake out all those pictures his words had created, a useless attempt to run away from the darkness in his voice. No charm in Ben Jackson's blunt words, only that darkness that carried her down on a river of sound. "A job. That's all I need." She clung to reality. "I *need* this job."

"I know." He touched the vein throbbing in her temple. "In the meantime, Annie, don't worry about it," he said, throwing her own words back to her. "We'll manage. I don't intend to let any more *accidents* happen between us. Because, sweet Annie, I know it's a no-win situation. Not for you, not for me."

There was nothing else to say.

She lacked an ability to move into prosaic chitchat.

The silence should have been uncomfortable.

It was.

For her, at any rate.

Driving steadily on, his hands relaxed and easy on the wheel, Ben seemed so unaffected that, as the miles moved in a silvery strip under the truck, she began to think that all the discomfort was on her side, that all the awareness was buzzing in her alone, began to think she'd imagined everything in some heated fantasy of despair and need.

And then he turned and smiled, a knowing, rueful smile.

Maybe it was just as well that the sexual revolution had passed her by. Annie stared out the passenger window and watched for her car.

If Annie hadn't murmured, "There it is," Ben wouldn't have seen the outline of her car. It had been moved farther into the shrubs at the side of the road. He frowned and guided the truck to a stop.

Gabe had called earlier in the day to arrange for a tow truck to bring Annie's car to the Star, but Barney had said he couldn't get to it until the day after Christmas. Saying he didn't think it was a good idea to leave the angel's chariot abandoned that long, Gabe had rummaged in the garage until he'd found heavy chains and jerry-rigged a way to fasten Annie's car to the truck.

Annie hadn't asked Ben to drive her back to the car, he'd volunteered. If he hadn't offered, he thought sourly, switching off the truck ignition, Gabe would have volunteered him—or worse, the old rooster would've swaggered off to tow the "angel's chariot" himself.

Ben saw the popped trunk lid before Annie did. Glancing around at the quiet woods, he remained in the truck, his hand stilling her quick movement for the door. "Wait."

He didn't like this. Something had happened here during the night. Nothing nice, no peace on earth, no good will in the gap between trunk lid and automobile.

Listening for sounds that didn't belong, he heard Annie's agitated breathing, the *scree* of an owl.

"Okay. Let's see what we have."

"What's wrong?" Her slim, cold fingers brushed his hand. "You look so—*violent.*"

He didn't know what she meant. He opened the truck door slowly, not taking his eyes off her car several feet away.

"Ben," she said as she grabbed his arm, "what's wrong?"

Real terror in the way she held on to him. Through his shirt sleeve, he could feel her hand shaking.

"I don't know." Still checking the roadside, he hesitated for a moment and said as he started to shut the door, not looking back to her, "Lock it."

But she'd been too quick, darting out behind him, her small hand still grasping his sleeve. "No. I can't do that."

"Too bad." Ben lifted her with one arm around her slim waist and swung her in front of him where he could see her.

When he'd left with Annie, he'd wanted Will and Katie to come with them as a buffer between him and their mother, but now he was glad that the children had remained with Gabe. "Stay close to me."

"Of course I will." Her shaky chuckle was terror-driven but game. "I'm not about to let you out of my sight when you're acting like a hound dog on point."

"I didn't know you hunted," he murmured, moving her forward, her fanny bumping his fly as he kept his arm around her while he stared at the blackness under her car, its darkened interior.

"I don't," she said through chattering teeth. "But I've been listening to Gabe all day."

"Bad habit. He'll corrupt you."

"Or the kids." Her narrow shoulders were shaking as he placed his hands on them, guiding her in the direction of the car while he kept a constant lookout. "He's got the kids singing some version of 'Jingle Bells' that keeps Will snickering like crazy and covering his mouth."

"That's Gabe." Ben dropped his hands and stepped to Annie's side. The person who'd popped the lid of her car hadn't lingered. Looking at a trail of red bows lying on the ground at the far side of the car, Ben decided if he could wrap his hands around the neck of the s.o.b. who'd vandalized Annie Conroy's belongings, he'd probably kill him.

Her "oh" was a shocked whimper. She'd seen the trunk and the bows.

Pity, unfamiliar and disturbing with its implications, whipped through him. Annie Conroy shouldn't have to cope with one more hardship. With everything he'd learned about her since she'd walked into his life, he knew she had courage to spare, but everyone had a breaking point, he thought, watching her drop to her knees beside the box of upended bows, three trailing from her hand.

"Oh." She looked up at him, her eyes blank and dry, "My Christmas bows." Opening her hands, she let the ribbons fall to the ground. "We'd managed to save them. Funny, isn't it? Katie salvaged them from the trash outside the apartment before we left." Her laugh was too high, its tension corkscrewing up as she choked out, "Have you ever seen anything so *funny*!'' In the twilight, her blue blouse shimmered around her shaking shoulders.

He'd never offered comfort to a woman.

Sex, pleasure, he'd offered and provided those frequently over the years.

But never comfort. He didn't know how to comfort, but, faced with Annie's agony, he hunched down beside her, carefully not touching her.

He didn't know how to comfort her, but he knew that if he touched her, she would fall apart, and Annie, gutsy, hopeful Annie who'd trekked her children and her Christmas bows this far without giving up, oh, she'd hate that, Annie would.

He tucked one of the bows into her twitching hands.

He wished she would cry. This dry-eyed, shaking Annie was terrifying him, her desolation running deep and dreadful.

Picking up a second bow, he folded it into her hands.

Then, while she knelt on the cool ground, Ben walked around the car, picking up red Christmas bows and carrying them back to her, dropping them like flowers on her lap while she watched him, her cloudy blue eyes dry, dry, and burning on him.

When he'd picked up all the bows, he hunkered down beside her again, his shoes touching the toes of her black leather flats. "Come on, Annie. We'll take everything back to the Star."

"All right." She held the hem of her skirt like a basket, the bows heaped inside its folds. "All right."

He hadn't believed Annie Conroy's bright voice would ever be dull and colorless. But it was, and he missed that brightness, missed the glow of her teasing cheerfulness and sass, craved the radiance that surrounded her like an aureole.

She walked beside him to the truck, head down, her fists clutching the hem of her skirt to her. Leaning against the fender, she waited while he carried what was left of her belongings from the car to his truck.

"I don't know what's missing. A lot of boxes were ripped open, but some weren't touched. The vandals must have been interrupted. They didn't take everything."

"All right," she repeated.

"Let me hook up the truck, and we'll tow the car back to Gabe."

"All right," she whispered, and this time Ben saw her rub her nose with the back of her wrist, her skirt lifting and falling with the movement of her hands death-wrapped around the skirted bows.

She didn't protest as he lifted her into the truck and brushed the heavy curtain of her hair back from her face, smoothing it so that she could see him.

Dangling from the cab, her bare knees were eye level to him, and, unbearably moved by their naked vulnerability, he covered them with a pleated edge of her skirt, his palms resting on top. "Annie, listen to me. Gabe will fix your car. He's a mechanic. Well, he used to be. Before he retired to run the bar. You're going to be all right."

"Am I? It's Christmas, Ben, and the presents are in Chicago under a dying tree." Her voice trembled and caught. "Am I going to be all right?" she murmured, her voice finally breaking, and he rested his forehead against her knees, his heart aching for her as memories of other Christmases drifted down over him like sea foam tossed in the wind.

Joy to the world and broken dreams.

All those shining expectations like shattered ornaments on a floor.

God, he hated the holidays.

He couldn't give her empty promises. With her courage, she deserved more from him than glib assurances.

Sliding her over and shutting the door to the truck, Ben went back to work, aware in every atom of his being of Annie in his truck as he sorted out the mess the vandals had made of her possessions.

Reasoning that she wouldn't want to inventory her suitcases and boxes tonight, he tried to identify the ones that contained clothes that she and Will and Katie would need for the next few days, making sure that those went into his truck. The rest of the boxes and cases he put back into her car.

When he was finished, he backed the truck up to the front of her car and worked Gabe's tow chains through the bumper supports, fastening the chains in two places to his truck so that Annie could remain with him in the truck and wouldn't have to steer her car on the way back.

The two vehicles joined together, Ben climbed into the truck and buckled Annie's seat belt around her. The need to comfort her ran through him still and he sat staring ahead into the tropical darkness, the reflection of Annie's car hood in his rearview mirror looming above him. Stiff-spined, she was silent, frozen next to him until he turned suddenly and wrapped his hand around the nape of her neck. "This isn't the end of the world, Annie. I don't know diddly about kids in general, but I know those two kids of yours don't care about the car, about their presents, not really."

She was listening. He could tell. The blankness lifted from her eyes as she came back to him from wherever she'd been hiding.

He brushed her hair back from her ears and the star earrings tinkled, a tiny chime in the quiet of the truck cab. With his forefinger, he stirred the earring on her left ear and heard again that faint chiming like faraway church bells.

The delicate lobe of her small ear was as soft as peach skin. Setting the stars ringing again, he said, "Come on, Annie. Let's go home."

At the lift of her chin, he realized what he'd said.

Home. When had he started thinking of the Star as *home?*

"You're right. Christmas is more than those presents."
Her wrist brushed the end of her tip-tilty nose again. "I was
being silly."

"I didn't say you were silly."

"Maybe not," she conceded, music coming into her
husky voice. "But I didn't have to make such a big deal out
of a bunch of bows."

But he noticed that she still held them enclosed in the
protection of her skirt.

"Well—" He shrugged. They'd seemed like a big deal to
him, too, when he'd seen her kneeling among the upheaval
of her belongings.

"But I had such *plans* for this Christmas." She paused,
and Ben knew the moment she started making new plans.
"I'll have to think what we can do. You said some of the
boxes and suitcases hadn't been touched?"

He nodded.

A light switched on inside her, and Gabe's angel-Annie
came back to life, her glow growing brighter with the passing miles.

When he lifted her out of the truck onto the parking lot,
she never turned loose of the ribbons. Carrying them
around to the back door, she took each ribbon out and
carefully straightened the crumpled edges before lining up
the bows along a row of cardboard boxes. "Katie won't
notice they're a little worse for wear. Will might, though."

"Yeah." Ben ran his finger along the ends of one satin
ribbon.

She sighed. "Don't say anything to the kids. Please. I
don't think they need to know about this last catastrophe."
Her laugh was strained, but she'd laughed, her soft lips
lifting in an honest-to-God-for-real smile that made its way
into her eyes as she regarded him. Tilting her head, she said
ironically, "Bet you're glad you were open last night, aren't
you, Ben Jackson? Think of all the excitement you would
have missed if we'd wandered on down the road."

Dirt smudged her nose and chin.

"Come here, Annie." Ben looped his finger under her narrow black belt and tugged. She did, walking right into his arms and laying her cheek over his heart.

"Thank you, Ben," she whispered into his shirt.

Unable to resist, he lifted her arms and pulled them around his waist, holding her to him with one hand while he wiped the smudges off her nose and chin with his other, using the cuff of his shirt as a washcloth.

"Just don't spit on it," she mumbled against him.

"What?" He leaned away from her fragrance and softness.

"It's a mom thing," she said. Her hair swung against his wrist and back, and her earrings tinkled. "When there's no water and your child has a spot on her face."

"Oh. I see." Leaning forward, he applied himself diligently to one stubborn spot at the corner of her mouth. "I won't spit."

"Thank you, thank you, thank you." She tightened her arms around him and he wanted to stay in the storeroom that way forever, Annie locked against him, her satin hair smooth against his mouth, her star earrings tinkling and chiming, chiming around him and filling him with a distantly remembered and longed-for music.

Chapter Six

Gabe winked at Annie as she walked into the bar. "Ben manage to tow your car back?"

"He's unchaining it now. I wanted to see whether or not Katie and Will gave you any trouble." She thought the old man seemed tired despite his impudent grin. "I was afraid that they might have worn you out."

"Huh, not a bit. That Will's a corker, I'll tell you. If he asked me one question, he must have asked a thousand. Wanted to know why if parts of Florida are below sea level, we're not walking around with the Gulf of Mexico and the Atlantic up to our ankles." He handed her a plate with a hamburger on it. "Thought you and Ben would be hungry." Forestalling her question, he added, "I fed the cherubs. They're upstairs in your room watching an old TV I found out in the garage. Black-and-white, but it works. Besides, *Miracle on Thirty-fourth Street* isn't in color, anyway."

"Thanks, Gabe." She took a bite out of the hamburger. "Gosh, this really is good."

"I know," he said smugly. "Didn't you wonder why we had a roomful of people way out here in the woods?"

Scanning the room, Annie realized he hadn't exaggerated. The tables were filled with people. "Good grief, Gabe," she exclaimed. "I shouldn't have let Katie and Will talk me into letting them stay here. I had no idea." She was bewildered. Last night the bar had been empty. "How did you manage by yourself?"

"Didn't." He uncorked a bottle of red wine and filled a glass with the ruby liquid. Pointing the cork at a tall white-haired man stooping over the grill, Gabe called, "Josh, here's the angel I was telling you about."

The man looked over his shoulder at Annie. "Hey there, Miss Annie. Shoot. I mean *Ms.* Annie. I don't have the hang of these newfangled, politically correct manners yet, but I'm working on it."

"Josh is a part-time professor over to the community college in Azalea. He's from *Dee*-troit—"

"Not anymore." Leaning closer to the grill, Josh mashed one burger with the spatula. He was older-looking than Gabe's seventy-three years, but moved gracefully despite the extra weight he carried.

Undeterred, Gabe continued, "But he's trying to blend in with the locals. Fifteen years now, and he's almost southern. 'Bout another five ought to do it, *I* reckon." He snorted maliciously. "He's a damn Yankee, but I forgive him. He couldn't help where he was born."

Using the spatula, Josh lifted a burger up to the light coming from the grill hood. "Nice to meet you, Ms. Annie, but I got no time to visit. I got a grill full of burgers and they're one minute from being ready for that table of six over there. This cooking business is serious work." His plump stomach bumped against the grill knobs. "Dang-nab it, Gabe. I keep forgetting this is such a small galley."

"Josh fancies himself a nautical man," Gabe said loudly. "He has a fiberglass rowboat with an outboard."

"This space was never meant to be a kitchen. You ever going to spring for a renovation on this kitchen area, Gabe?" he rumbled as he flipped a burger onto a prepared bun.

"Talk to Ben. He's the money man, but, personally speaking, I like my kitchen the way it is. Plenty big enough for *me*," Gabe said innocently.

Josh glowered.

Ready to grab for a tray and hustle hamburgers over to the table of six, Annie was astounded as one more elderly man bellied up to the bar.

"Here you go, Mike. Three pink cows, one red, and two black." Josh shoved the plates heaping with fries and burgers over to the gray-haired man standing quietly next to her.

Until Josh spoke, she'd thought the gray-haired man was just a customer.

"Hello, Mrs. Conroy. I'm Mike Hanlon. I've met your children. Delightful infants." He dipped his graying head politely in her direction as he placed the plates onto the tray he'd been holding by his side.

Unless Annie missed her guess, by the cut and fabric of his elegant suit, Mike was wearing an Armani. Or a suit in a similar price range. She'd worked one year in the courthouse gofering for the lawyers, and she'd learned to recognize expensive suits. She stared and knew her mouth was open.

As if he'd read her mind, Gabe nodded. "Yep. Mike's a sometimes-lawyer. Sometimes he doesn't win, sometimes he loses." Gabe chortled.

"Thank you, Gabriel, for that addition to the humor of the evening. I'm sure Mrs. Conroy appreciates your wit." Mike walked to the table of people waiting for their meals, and handed the plates around the circular table with an economy of motion that indicated familiarity with the process.

He'd waited tables here before.

"You don't need a waitperson, do you, Gabe?" Annie scraped the edge of the bar. She'd been afraid his offer was charity and had decided she didn't care, but being slapped in the face with the obvious was harder to handle than she'd expected.

"These old goats?" Gabe scoffed. "Hell's bells, angel, one night at the Star's about all they're good for. Damn right we need you here. You came at closing time last night. The supper crowd had gone, and the drinkers were winding down." He leaned over the bar toward her, rising on his tiptoes. "I know this place *looks* like a juke joint, but it ain't. You don't think I'd have let you and the cherubs stay here if that's what we were, do you?"

"I don't know, Gabe." Sinking onto a bar stool, Annie dropped her head into her hands. "And, to tell you the truth, I don't care, either." She smiled up at him through parted fingers as his watery eyes squinted. "I'm grateful for your help. Thank you."

And she was. She, who'd never asked for help, never wanted to accept it from anyone, had been helped at every turn since she'd seen that flickering green star.

And she'd never needed help more.

"Why don't you go check on the cherubs? Come on back down after you've settled a spell. The evening's young, even if me and Mike and Josh ain't." Gabe shooed her away from the bar with hand motions. "And take this orange juice." He handed her a waxed carton. "Katie-did looks like she could use a solid dose of vitamin C."

Holding the slippery carton in her hands, Annie started to cry, all the tears she hadn't shed when she'd seen the last of her possessions strewn across the sandy soil dripping silently down her cheeks. She tasted their salt at the corner of her mouth.

At Gabe's worried frown, she reached for the black metal napkin holder and yanked out a handful of coarse paper napkins. Clutching the orange juice carton to her chest, she blotted her eyes and stood up. Afraid she would become a puddle of all the tears she'd been holding back for weeks if she didn't get out of Gabe's sight immediately, she mumbled, "I'll come right back down, guys," and fled.

At the bottom of the stairs, she sat down and blew her nose, wadding up the rough paper and stuffing it into her skirt pocket where it joined a roll of hard candies she carried for Will.

With her head bent, she saw Ben's shoes first, the glossy tips at the edge of her vision. Not looking up, she said, "Do you want me to unload my car now?"

"No. I carried the stuff from the truck up to your room. What's in the car can stay there until you need it. It won't be in Gabe's way when he's working on the car." A polished shoe tip bumped the toe of her black shoe. "I see you met the wise guys."

"Oh, yes." Annie moved her feet to one side, making room for Ben to go upstairs. "Quite a crew you have working for you, Mr. Jackson."

"The guys are Gabe's friends. Not mine."

"No?" She slid her feet to one side again, silently offering him an invitation to leave, hoping he would.

"They hang out here. You're apt to find them chugging down coffee and pickled eggs at seven in the morning before they head out to fish."

"Mike fishes?" Annie wondered how five-hundred-dollar suits held up to sun and salt.

"Yeah. They all do. Mike and Josh have retired and made the Star their second home. They've been here as long as I have. Fact is, I think they came with the bar."

"Expensive accessories." Behind the curtain of her hair, Annie sneaked a quiet honk into a napkin.

Playing tag, Ben's shoe nudged her foot. "Annie, come on. Look at me."

"No."

"Afraid the sight of your red-rimmed eyes will inflame me with savage passion, are you?" he taunted. One gray-clad knee came into her field of view.

"Of course."

His other knee rested against the stair riser, and she felt the slow brush of his hand through her hair, swooping it back from her face. "Afraid I'll think you're a sissy?"

She nodded and ducked her head away from him.

"Hey, Annie. Aren't you up-to-date? Even boys get to cry in the nineties."

"I know." She moved her knees and feet sideways until she faced the wall.

"Everybody gets to be a sissy now and then without having to feel like a failure." His voice lowered and his face dipped close to hers until she couldn't avoid his gaze any longer. "Even you, Annie."

"I know."

He was nose-to-nose with her. "You've had a long day."

"A *really* long day."

His nose bumped hers. "Go see Katie and Will. Take a hot shower. Go to bed."

Closing her fingers around the ball of napkins and candies, she swallowed. "I have a job to do. You can't send me to bed. I'm your waitperson, not a child."

Gripping her elbow, he lifted her to face the landing at the top of the stairs. "Fine. Come back down, but don't drop the juice on your way upstairs, Annie," he jeered gently as she swayed on the step. "No more *accidents,* remember?"

Two steps higher than he was, she became the same height as he, the orange juice carton between them, their knees touching, their breaths mingling. "Right," she said and turned away.

Leaving Ben at the bottom of the stairs, she went to her children.

"Mommy!" Katie leaped at her. "You're home!"

"And look what Gabe sent you." She held up the carton, once more grateful, this time to have something to distract them from questions she didn't want to answer. She pointed to the beer mugs on the plastic tray beside Will. "What did you drink?"

"Milk. Gabe said we needed—" he frowned "—calcium." Will picked up the mugs. "I'll rinse them in the bathroom, right?"

"Terrific." She walked with him to the doorway. Stooping, she said, "Were you all right while I was gone?"

He clinked the mugs together and, hearing the sound of glass against glass, turned his mouth upside down in a grimace of anxiety. "I didn't break them." His eyes were enormous.

"Of course not. Bar mugs are indestructible."

"Except in the movies."

"Well, the *movies*," she said scornfully, eyeing the mugs for cracks. "*Nothing's* real in the movies."

"The actors are," he said seriously. Glancing at Katie, Will whispered, "This movie's all about Santa Claus, but I didn't say anything to her. I wouldn't ruin Christmas for her, Mommy, especially when we're in the soup."

"I know, sweetheart." Annie kissed the top of his head. "Go rinse the mugs, Will. You've been a big help to me these last weeks." She tugged his ear. "But you always are."

"You count on me," he said.

"Of course I do. I don't know what I'd do without you or Katie—"

"Katie's a baby. I watched her all afternoon so she wouldn't be any trouble for Gabe. We have to take care of *her.* She can't help."

"Yes, but—" Annie bent down, trying to ease the load he'd decided he had to carry. "Will, you love Katie, right?"

He nodded. "But babies are different. Everybody loves babies. *I* am not a baby."

"Sweetheart, we love her because she's *Katie,* not because she's my baby. And I love you because you're *Will.* You don't have to earn my love, sweetheart. We don't love people because of what they do for us."

"Daddy never helped." Will's eyes were astute and held a knowledge she wished he'd never learned.

"No. He didn't."

"You don't love him anymore." Will held the mugs up to the light, studying the milky white film inside. "You told him so. I heard you. You told him he never took responsibility for anything."

"I know I said that, but—"

"I am *very* responsible." He lowered the mugs and trotted out.

When Will returned with the rinsed mugs, Annie sat tailor-style on the floor with them, while they drank. Katie crawled into her lap and lay with her arms around Annie's waist. Watching the movie and its fictional Santa, Katie sat up until her rosebud mouth was close to Annie's ear and lisped, "Santa Claus will find us here. Gabe said so." Like steam, her *s* sounds puffed at Annie's ear.

Ben had been right.

The children didn't care about presents. They needed her, they needed the stability of her in control and coping with life. She'd forgotten that truth for those few awful minutes at the side of the road until Ben had spelled it out for her.

It might not be what she'd planned, but she could give Katie her Christmas, give Will a chance to remember for a while that he was only seven years old.

"I will write Santa a letter and leave milk. Gabe said I could," Katie said, making plans of her own.

Annie closed her eyes. There *had* to be something salvageable in the remaining boxes. She could make do.

She would keep coping.

One way or another.

On the way to his room, Ben heard Katie's lisp and paused. The childish confidence in myths overwhelmed him. How could Annie bear up under the weight of those innocent expectations, day after day?

A single parent, she carried the burden of her children's wistful longings alone, her slim shoulders the entire support of their world. He'd said that to her, but he hadn't understood, not until this moment how solitary a duty hers was, hadn't comprehended the scope of her pledge to her children.

Happy ever after. Till death us do part. Santa Claus. Myths.

Annie Conroy had constructed a house of straw for her children and left it unfortified, their trust and hope vulnerable to the winds of fate and reality.

He'd given her false comfort after all.

Stripping a clean pair of slacks out of the plastic covering, Ben unbuttoned a fresh shirt from its folds and carried his clothes with him to the bathroom.

Cleaning up as quickly as he could, he wiped down the shower and folded his dirty shirts and slacks for the trip to the cleaners when Christmas was finally over.

Slicking back his hair, he checked the supper crowd from behind the stained-glass window as he went downstairs. Business was even better than usual.

"Think you can fix Annie's car?" Ben stepped up behind Gabe and untied the old man's apron, wrapping it around himself as he strolled to the long mahogany counter. "Or were you tooting your own horn to impress a pretty lady?" He lifted a french fry from a plate Josh passed under his arm to Mike.

"*Annie,* is it?" Gabe grinned maliciously. "Old son, what happened out there? Somebody hit you in the head with a two-by-four and set you right?" He eased himself slowly onto a stool, his bones creaking as he lowered himself. "Of course I can fix it." He scowled at Ben. "Leastways I can once I know what broke on it."

"I wanted to know for sure. She thinks you can." Ben scratched his chin. "And I did something real stupid. I told her you could. She's counting on you."

"So?" The old man groaned as he stood up. "I can handle it, Ben. I'm not too old, and not too decrepit." His smile was pensive. "I can fix anything. You know that."

"Yeah. Well, she's counting on you," Ben said again, not sure why he needed to make sure Gabe wouldn't fail her. He shrugged.

"I know." Gabe patted his shoulder. "She is something special, ain't she, Ben?" Sidling past Josh, Gabe jabbed him in the ribs. "I'll see you in the morning. Try to leave some of the burgers for the customers."

"Rough night for Gabe?" Ben said casually as he stacked the clean plates away and emptied the dishwasher underneath the counter.

"He's old."

"I know." Ben lifted a load of dishes ready for the machine. A plate slipped, but he caught it one-handed, balancing the others against his hip. "But Gabe's... Well. I wondered, that's all." He rubbed his neck.

"We keep him under control. Of course he's not too happy about it." Josh smirked. "Gabe still thinks he's forty something." He wiped his hands down his greasy apron. "Nothing really wrong with him, though, except worn-out bones and the usual aches and pains that go along with being old and ornery. And Gabe Thibideaux is one ornery old man, that's for sure." Grease splattered Josh's arm. "Durn it. You're going to have to do something about making more room back here, Ben, if you plan on crowds like the ones you've had this last year."

"It's big enough for me."

Throwing his large head back in a roar of laughter, Josh boomed, "You've been hanging around the old man too long, Ben. He expressed the same sentiment in almost identical words."

"Yeah?" Ben allowed himself a small smile. "We're becoming a couple of old stick-in-the-muds, aren't we?"

"That's not news to anybody." Josh slid three more loaded plates down the wooden bar to Mike, who, stopping the plates with a tray, merely nodded and carried them off.

"I like the Star the way it is." Swinging the dishwasher lever on, Ben said. "That's why I bought it. I'm not looking to change the place. Hell, I might not even be here long enough to see the electricians through the first stage, and I wouldn't want to leave Gabe with a mess."

"No. You wouldn't do that to him." Josh was silent for a few minutes. "Gabe said he might go into Azalea for the holiday. He has a lady friend there, so he says. If you can believe him." Josh slid a T-bone onto a large platter. "Are you going down there with him?"

"He's bluffing. He was mad at me and hauled out Azalea Park as a threat. He's staying here." Nodding to the bluejeaned man at the end of the bar who held up one finger, Ben slid a beer down the shining length of the wood and said, "The bar will be open. Same as last year and the year before that. I'm not going to close for the day."

"I might mosey on over this way, then," Josh said, his beefy fingers overwhelming the toothpick he jammed into the top of the hamburger. "Set a spell if y'all don't mind."

Ben was amused. Josh's acquired drawl had returned, thick as syrup and reasonably authentic for a *Dee*-troit man. When it suited him, and it rarely did anymore, Josh spoke in the educated accents that revealed the years he'd spent teaching philosophy at his Michigan university. Most of the time, though, some perversity of humor made him delight in passing himself off as a backwoods cracker.

Not letting Josh see his smile, Ben said, "Suit yourself. I'm not going anywhere. Business as usual here." Ben started the dishwasher and flattened himself against the counter as Josh squeezed by to the storeroom.

"Good." Josh glanced at him. "I'll plan on it."

Watching his broad back, Ben wondered what Gabe had told his friend. Josh had never asked about Ben's background, never seemed surprised that the Star stayed open every holiday. Josh always checked before turning up at the bar, though.

Empty-handed, Josh stopped at the end of the counter. "You're out of pickles, Jackson."

"Yeah? You sure? There should be one jar of the small gherkins."

"If they're there, I didn't see them." Josh returned to the grill. "But nobody will miss them. Pickles are nothing more than these bumpy green things decorating the plate. They have no significance in the universal mystery of life. Pickles don't count. Kind of like the government labeling ketchup a vegetable in the school lunch programs a while back."

Ben laughed. "But I would have sworn we had enough to get us through the week. I remember thinking I'd have to reorder before New Year's." He raised an eyebrow at the crowd and glanced at Josh. "You reckon this is a pickle-thieving crowd? Think we ought to call the sheriff?"

Looking at the mix of faded jeans and jewelry, Josh grumbled, "Wouldn't hurt. These yuppy-puppies and cowboys are a strange mix. 'Course, they all wear jeans. I finally figured out that it's the lawyers from Palma de Flora, though, who're wearing the jeans with the holes. Mike agreed. Shoot-fire, these modern times are something." Josh shook his head. "I'm surprised you don't have a fight every night, but Gabe says you keep things in check." His glance was shrewd and knowing as he added, "Gabe says you like everything tidy and under control."

Surveying the white-haired older man, Ben wondered what point he was making. "Yeah. I do."

Josh turned back to the grill and ran the spatula over it, scraping bits and pieces of meat into the grease trough. "Ms. Annie's thrown you a curve ball, hasn't she?" Unwrapping eight more beef patties, Josh slapped them against the grill, grinning like a man who'd triple-jumped Ben's checkers.

Damn. The three old men were all alike.

They saw everything and never turned down a chance to zip in a zinger. To him, to one another. Whatever happened to old men sitting placidly on park benches? Ben reckoned he'd be first in line to buy up a truckload of benches if he could talk Mike, Josh and Gabe into slowing down long enough to plunk their assorted rear ends on a bench and stay out of his business.

Fed up with everybody butting in and picking around in his life, Ben felt the threads of his temper fraying and flapping. "Listen—" he snarled.

"And speaking of the lady—" Josh waggled the spatula toward the stairway entrance.

Wearing a red cotton sweater and black straight skirt that ended two inches above her knees, Annie was rounding the door frame, her hair swinging back and forth, gaudy red Christmas tree bulbs swaying from her ears. Transformed into earrings, the large, old-fashioned screw-in bulbs should have been tacky. Swaying in and out of the gloss of her hair, there was nothing subtle and understated about their glittery red and brass.

On Annie the silly earrings were beautiful.

Irresistibly cheerful, goofy, brave, they heralded her indomitable spirit to the world.

"I found the clean aprons," she said. Head down, she double-wrapped the ties around her waist and gave a final pull to the large bow she'd created. At the bottom, an inch of black skirt framed the white square. She flipped her hair back with both hands. Her cheeks were maraschino-red against her pale hands. "Ready, willing, reporting for duty.

And reasonably able." She smiled, a miracle of muscles and skin and spirit that was breathtaking in the small oval of her face.

Something deep inside him stirred and moved to the sound of her low, husky voice, twisted and shattered at the sight of her smile.

Oh, Annie, Ben thought, mute in the face of her bright courage. Annie.

"Where do you want me to start? Tables?" She tipped her head, scanning the room. "The grill? Drinks?" She glanced at him, and her voice became breathless as she saw him silently watching her. "Oh." Her mouth pursed and she stilled her lively movements.

"I'm happy as a pig in a mud hole. Expect you could relieve Mike." Breaking into the lengthening silence, drawl at its thickest, Josh saved Ben.

And with his grin let Ben know payment would be collected later. With interest.

Unable to take his gaze from Annie and her ridiculous earrings that were shattering his heart, Ben swallowed. "Yeah. Mike's been on his feet a while. He could use a break by now. Can you handle the tables?"

"Sure. I know where everything is. I think. Gabe showed me."

Even moving in slow motion, Annie was still faster than most people. Her hands flashed over stacked trays, pulling one out, a huge, silvery disk that shielded her from thigh to breastbone. With a saucy grin, she tacked on, "And yes, I know waiting tables isn't as easy as it looks, Mr. Jackson, sir."

"It's easy to confuse a tableful of food and drink orders," Ben cautioned. "Hungry people tend to get a tad snappish where food's concerned."

"I know." The twitch of her fanny in his direction was deliberately insolent and sassy. "Can't be dumb, slow and careless with the soup if you want good tips."

"You've waited tables, I reckon?"

"Until I was eight and a half months pregnant with Will, I bussed and waited tables wherever anyone would hire me." Her grin lost a measure of sass. "It's been a while since I've slung plates and carried loaded trays, but I can handle this crowd."

The sight of her long, bare legs shifting and dancing below the silver tray as she darted around Josh and scooted in front of Ben was a picture Ben thought he'd carry to his grave, long after Annie vanished somewhere down the road, leaving the Star behind her in the dust.

And him.

One more memory he'd carry with him and try to forget.

"Hey, Ms. Annie, what's going on with your tykes?"

"Gabe's showing them how to tie fish lures." She spun the tray like a hoop through her fingers and the silver metal flashed like the spinning wheel at the carnival.

Spin and win a prize.

Ben always had. Most he'd given away or pitched out before leaving the fairs and carnivals. But the hula doll had appealed to something whimsical in his eight-year-old self and he'd hung on to the battery-operated doll with her carny lights flashing around her skirt.

Over the years, he'd carted the blue-eyed, red-haired doll around with him from place to place, the only souvenir he'd kept.

He couldn't bring himself to throw it away.

"I promised I'd take the kiddos out in my boat before y'all leave. Reckon old Gabe's getting them ready."

A rippling rainbow of sound, her chuckle interrupted Ben's melancholy thoughts.

"They're tangled in nylon string and feathers right now. From what I saw, I can't imagine what kind of sea creature Katie will catch."

"Gabe will make sure they catch a fish if the weather cooperates. We'll see if we can work something out soon. According to the long-range forecast, we're due for a cold snap before New Year's.'' Josh grabbed a wood-handled fork as he ordered, ''Toss me a long-neck, Ben. I'm working up a thirst over this hot stove.''

Ben held a beer out to Josh, who reached for it while spearing a rib eye steak onto a second platter.

Before Josh could snag the bottle, Annie, tearing in front of Ben with the tray now over her head, brushed against his outstretched arm. Wrapped around the cold bottle, Ben's hand tingled at the slide of Annie's red-cottoned breast. Warm, supple. Annie-heat against his knuckles, ice on the flat of his palm. Startling and arousing, that fire and ice. His muttered ''sorry'' collided with hers, and then she was on the safe side of the bar.

Taking the beer a second too late, Josh downed half in one swallow.

Ben's empty hand burned with fire and ice and Annie's softness.

Watching her flee to a table as far away from the bar as she could find, her fanny a minute curve of black fabric against the voluminous white apron, Ben wanted to see her eyes and discover there the sizzling need he thought he'd sensed in her as she brushed past him.

Not safe, definitely not smart, but he craved it, needing to know that what he felt wasn't one-sided even if neither of them wanted that static electricity jumping from her to him, him to her, zinging back and forth, the sudden sting and crackle at the arc's completion.

Like magnets flying inevitably toward each other, he and Annie kept touching, their bodies drawn together beyond their wills.

Such a strange force, desire.

Freud was probably right.

No such thing as accidents.

But sexual chemistry, Ben decided, as he watched the mesmerizing twitch of Annie's behind flitting from table to table, oh, yes, that was an accident of flesh and scent.

And something more, something inexplicable and incomprehensible, that compelling magnet of one person for another.

Annie, sweet-faced, gutsy and foolishly optimistic, drew him with a power he couldn't understand.

She made him remember the past when all he wanted to do was forget it.

Ben opened a beer for himself and tipped it to his dry mouth as he watched Annie's graceful dance through the tables of the Star.

He knew why he'd kept the hula doll all those years.

Shaking her head, his mother had touched the skirt twinkling with lights, the doll's fire-engine red curls, and then she'd laughed, a lighthearted sound filled with amusement and love as she'd lifted him onto her lap and watched the miniature lights flash on and off, on and off, with each flick of the hula doll's ceramic hips. *On. Off.*

It was the last time he'd seen his mother smile.

Chapter Seven

If the man with the wafer-thin watch patted her fanny one more time, Annie intended to dump her next order of grease-rich fries into his lap and over his hundred-dollar, stone-washed jeans. To heck with the tip promised by his expensive cowboy boots. Scanning them scornfully, she knew they'd never seen the side of a horse.

Trailing her empty tray on the way to clean up a table, Annie gritted her teeth and smiled as Cowboy Bill motioned her over. His date, tall, gorgeous, and with legs an NBA basketball player would kill for, rolled her eyes and kicked him under the table, a kick not meant for Annie to see.

"Hey there, pretty lady," he said, as she approached. Tipping back on the legs of his chair, he gestured her closer, the better to trap her with his octopus arms, she'd decided much earlier in the evening.

But she was being unfair to the poor octopus, she concluded as she assessed the gleam in the cowboy's eyes.

"Yes?" Annie made a point of docking at the side of the cowboy's "little lady."

"Bring us another round of drafts, quick-quick, honey. And one more thing—" Still wiggling his hand, he motioned for her to come around the table to his side, and reached for the heavy ceramic bowl on the table.

"More dill pickles?" Taking the brown bowl, Annie stayed judiciously out of arm's length, but he grabbed the bottom of her apron and jerked her toward him. Stumbling, she swung her tray in front of her, thwacking his wrist. "Oh, I'm *so* sorry, *sir,*" she said worriedly. "I must have slipped."

Cowboy Bill rubbed his wrist and scowled, not sure exactly what had happened.

With her most innocent smile, Annie placed the chunky bowl on the tray. "Gosh, let me get you some fresh pickles right away. Are you okay?"

His date patted his hand. "He's *so-o-o* tough. He'll be fine."

Stifling a giggle, Annie wondered if anyone else had heard the curl of sarcasm in the redhead's dulcet tones.

Striding to Cowboy Bill's table, Ben halted Annie, his broad palms braceleting her upper arms. Surprised, she skidded, her heel slipping on a wet spot of beer, and smashed into his chest, her nose banging up against his midsternum. Barricading her there out of view of the tables, Ben wouldn't let her skip past him to the bar.

"Pickles," she gasped, inhaling. And over the smell of cigarettes, beer and frying hamburgers, she smelled Ben, the starchy-fresh smell of his shirt filling her lungs, and something else there, too, something dark speaking to her out of his clean fragrance, something that made her want to press closer and closer and right into his darkness. Against her heated face, the slickly finished surface of the cotton was cool and hard. "He wants more pickles with his beer."

"Pickles?" Ben scowled at the table of four, narrowing in on Cowboy Bill, and then his ticked-off gaze returned to Annie, aggression radiating from him so strongly that she leaped back despite his grip on her arms, and he followed, moving right into her space, and he was too close and not nearly close enough. "What's he want with more pickles?" Releasing her, Ben plunked the bowl on the bar. His mouth thinned as he regarded the unfortunate urban cowpoke a few yards away dolefully rubbing his wrist. "We're out. Tell him to go somewhere else if he wants pickles."

"Ben." Stretching up on her toes and keeping a careful distance between her yearning self and the slick, hard surface of Ben Jackson's ironed shirt, Annie murmured, "He's a toad. But, despite any expectations he may harbor, he's not going to turn into a prince with my help." She glanced over her shoulder at the redhead. "And I think he's out of luck with her, too, poor baby," she cooed.

Ben's scowl deepened as he glared at her. "It's not funny, Annie. I saw what happened."

"I know you did." She pointed to the back of her neck. "I have a spot right here where a hole's been burning through me for the past twenty minutes. I know how to handle jerks like him and salvage a tip. Really." She flipped her hair away from her nape.

"Yeah. I reckon you can." He put her behind him and gave her an easy shove toward the bar. "But I'm going to have a chat with Romeo of the Roving Hands." Easy as the slide of oil over a hot skillet, Ben strolled over to the cowboy.

His brooding belligerence touched her.

On her account, he was ready to go to war with the cowboy.

She didn't see what happened, only that the cowboy was suddenly on his feet with Ben's arm draped buddy-buddy style over the man's shoulder.

Followed by his date, Bill was leaving. Casual, friendly, arm still resting on the cowboy's shoulder, Ben escorted him to the door.

Annie thought the tight pinch of Ben's grip on the man's neck probably had something to do with the cowboy's docile exit.

It had been a long, long time since anyone had been ready to come to her defense.

Even a woman with a working car, a three-bedroom apartment and cash in the bank could become addicted to the kind of comfort Ben's solid presence offered.

What chance did she have, with no safety net and nothing but ox-stubborn determination to keep herself, Will and Katie going? She was too vulnerable to Ben Jackson's starchy-clean smell and his rugged frame. She'd been without a shoulder to lean on for so long, and his shoulders were broad and strong. Resisting that rocklike security could sap the last ounce of her energy.

She was much too vulnerable to the loneliness she saw in his tough face.

Surrender, no matter how tempting, would be a denial of everything she'd accomplished since she was eighteen years old and picking wedding rice out of her hair.

Love was like a seesaw. It worked best when the players were equal.

Ben Jackson was a reluctant knight, and she a most unwillingly rescued fair maiden.

Watching the width of his back as he stood holding the door of the Star open, Annie felt humor bubbling in her. Did having two children and a divorce decree classify her as a rescued fair matron?

She didn't like either image of herself, maiden or matron hanging around waiting for rescue.

As the commercial made clear, a man's gotta do what a man's gotta do. Annie made a face. She'd learned it worked both ways.

All the fairy tales and myths ended when a girl grew up, and a woman had to do what a woman had to do.

Too bad for that woman if she had a lingering sense of loss, a longing to curl against someone and rest, if only for a moment. Too bad if the woman sometimes had a yearning for happy endings and miracles.

Annie sighed and loaded her tray with catsup and steak sauce and leaned over the bar for a stack of the napkins.

She'd been helped enough for one day.

Time to crawl back up on the tightwire and do her balancing act, safety net or not.

Checking the clock on the wall behind the bar, she took a deep breath. One more hour.

Sensing Ben in back of her, she shuffled the napkins and sauce bottles, arranging them in a triangle and then back to a soldierly battle line.

"Tired?" Cool and reserved, Ben's deep voice wove around her, but she didn't turn to look at him.

"No." Even with her back to him, she'd known the minute he was two feet away. Concentrating, she dipped into a large glass jar and spooned out slippery pickled eggs into one bowl, filled another with popcorn. "You've been busy tonight. Who waits table when the wise guys aren't handy?"

Clasped in Ben's hand, a basket of fried onions slipped onto the tray. "Gabe cooks. I see to tables, tend bar. People wait."

"They wait?" Grabbing the plates Josh slid toward her, she added them to the tray and took a breath, girding herself for a face-to-face with the man at her back.

His smile was self-mocking. "It's the charm of the Star."

"I can't believe you can get away with making people wait for their food."

"They reckon the longer the lines, the better the food. You know how people are. Everybody likes to discover some hole-in-the-wall. And that's what the Star has become.

We've been the flavor of the month for eighteen months, and word-of-mouth brings us our customers.''

She could feel his breath slide against her neck.

He was crowding her. He was too close to her back.

Annie turned and braced herself against the bar edge as she lifted the tray to her shoulder.

Big mistake. Air whooshed out of her lungs, and she felt her arms tremble under the weight of the tray, under the impact of his sardonic half smile.

Two feet clear of her, not crowding her at all, he leveled the tray for her and stepped ostentatiously aside. ''Okay? Tray's not too much for you?''

''Certainly not,'' she babbled. The world was whipping in a dizzying spin around her while she stood with the ground rocking and dissolving into pieces under her feet.

A breeze lifting the leaves and fluttering them, his awareness of her confusion moved through his final question and fluttered against her arms, raising goose bumps.

His tuned-in perception was unnerving.

Grabbing the tray with both hands, she fled.

Watching Annie wend her way through the tables and customers during the last hour the Star stayed open, Ben found to his dismay that, unerringly, every time he looked up from washing glasses, filling a mug, or ringing change from the cash register, he hunted Annie. Found her to the side of the room wiping a table, sensed her Annie-sweetness as she dipped around him and snatched a glass of water, saw her frivolous light-bulb earrings glinting and shining from the shimmering surface of the mirror.

At ten-thirty when the final two customers dropped their napkins beside their plates and the room was empty except for the four of them, Ben saw Annie's shoulders sag. Rotating her neck, she bent over and touched her toes, letting her head drop to the floor. Below the border of her black skirt, the backs of her knees were pale, mysterious, the backs of her calves a long curve to the fine bones of her ankles.

Wanting to run his palms over that vulnerable swoop of skin, the elegant arc of her fanny, unable to look away, Ben saw Mike pause in front of her.

The old lawyer's words carried to Ben.

Patting her on the back on his way to the bar stools, Mike laughed. "Mrs. Conroy, you have to learn to slow down. One of the benefits of age is learning to pace oneself. Pacing also works when one is less than seventy. Perhaps you might consider it a conservation effort?"

The cape of Annie's satiny hair settled around her face as she swept upright, and the flex of her long spine was a marvel of skin and bones. "I have a hard time sitting still, Mr. Hanlon. And I love the way the world looks from the whirl-i-gig. Besides, there's always so much to do." Smoothing her hair flat, she laughed, and, as she pivoted and saw Ben watching and listening as he had all night, her face flushed that delicate, infinitely intriguing pink.

"Sitting and watching the scenery is permissible. You wouldn't break one of the Ten Commandments, Mrs. Conroy, if you slowed down to thirty-three-and-a-third."

Already moving toward the bar, she laughed again. "Is that the southern way?" She pushed a bar stool under the bar. "Sounds appealing."

Caught by the dimmed lights around the bar, her hair swung forward against the pale, smooth skin of her neck. Ben wiped the bar, folding and refolding the towel as he polished and burnished, each long stroke down the glossy wooden surface an inadequate substitute for the slide of her heavy hair under his palms, for the touch of that smooth skin against his mouth.

He moved away from her and toward Mike.

Mike handed Ben his apron, order pad and tray. "Before air-conditioning, we southerners lived to the pace of nature, and I've discovered as I grow older a nostalgia for that life. The nineties move at a pace too frenetic for me. I long for the days when I left my front door ajar, the screen door unlocked and my windows wide-open all night long to the smell of orange blossoms and night-blooming jasmine.''

As Annie edged past Ben to the under-the-counter refrigerator, her own fragrance drifted to him with her quick movements back and forth. Her scent came to him from the swing of her hair, from the warm heat of her silky arms flashing in and out of his sight, from *her,* as seductive and inescapable as the drifting scent of gardenias and magnolias in a sultry night.

"I miss those days, Mrs. Conroy." Sadness rippled in Mike's cultured accent, and Ben heard Mike's loneliness not only for a way of life that had outstripped him, but also for the long-gone people who'd made up that life.

"I'm sure you do, Mr. Hanlon." Stilled, Annie tilted her head in sympathy. "Christmas brings back a lot of memories, doesn't it?" She touched his hand gently. "I'm sorry."

"Don't be, Mrs. Conroy. Life has its cycles, and now, though I may not sleep with my dear wife, Beatrice, by my side and my windows wide-open, nevertheless I'm still able to go out on my porch and listen to the mockingbirds in the early dawn and think about the past. My ghosts keep me company in the long twilights. I have wonderful memories.''

Listening to Mike's still-firm voice recalling his youth, Ben knew he'd always remember *this* moment, Annie's fragrance coming to him like a current of light eddying through the darkness of the familiar smells of the Star.

He knew with a soul-searing certainty that no matter how old he grew, no matter what else he forgot in the remaining years of his life, the remembered scent of Annie Conroy would always bring with it a bittersweet pang.

Mike eased himself up onto the bar stool. "However, casting nostalgia aside, dear lady, between dawn and twilight, I have a long journey home." Folding his lean, elegant hands in front of him, he said, nodding toward Ben. "Mr. Jackson and Mr. Thibideaux keep me busy with their legal needs, and I have other local clients who depend on me. While one would prefer to hibernate and 'just say no,' it occurs to me at this point in my life that saying yes makes my existence more interesting and the twilights more sweet."

Leaning toward Mike, Annie kissed his cheek. "Merry Christmas, Mr. Hanlon."

"Thank you." The aristocratic dip of his chin indicated that the time for nostalgia had ended. "Ben." Mike templed his fingers.

Untying the bow of her too-big apron, Annie zipped around the corner to the stairs. "I'll be back to clean up. I want to check on Katie and Will." Without her, the room was darker, seedier.

"Yes, Mike?" Ben leaned against the now-cool grill. He would let the old gentleman approach the subject in his own way.

"Although I don't mean to create an awkward situation for you, I wondered whether the Star would be open on Christmas Day?" Index fingers tapping, elegant eyebrows raised, Mike waited.

"Sure." Ben folded his arms.

"Ah. I'll file that information away for reference, then, should I find myself at loose ends." Sliding off the stool, Mike nodded as he said, "Quite an interesting evening, Ben. Tell Gabe I'll see him."

Mike walked out the front door and Ben locked the door behind him.

Even if he'd changed his mind and decided to close for the day, Ben could see he was going to have to keep the doors unlocked. Mike, like Josh, had no relatives nearby to spend the day with. While Ben's only intention in keeping the bar open had been simply to avoid the trappings of the holiday, Mike, Josh and Gabe were creating their own holiday observance.

They were falling into a pattern. Next thing he knew, they'd expect to exchange presents.

Time to move on.

He would sell out his share of the bar and pack up for greener pastures.

California. Maine.

Somewhere besides here where three old men, Annie *and* her children were beginning to make him feel very crowded.

Footloose and fancy-free was what he needed. He didn't need this ragtag collection of souls drifting in like white sand-dust around him. What he needed was somewhere else, not here, not when he'd begun thinking of the Star as home.

Running his forefinger under his shirt neck, Ben tugged at his collar.

The Star was nothing more than a pile of claptrap boards, a building. A roadhouse bar that served hamburgers.

Temporary.

Australia. Big surf. Wallabies. Time to see another part of the big old world.

He didn't need the hassle of liquor permits, inspections and vanishing jars of gherkins.

Time to move on and shake the dust from his shoes. After the holidays. In a month or two.

He went to get the cleaning supplies. Gabe hadn't returned, but Ben was content. This was the part of the night he liked. The quiet, dark room with its smells, its peaceful darkness. He wiped down the tables and checked the supplies at each one, readying the tables for the next day.

Christmas Eve.

The rattle of the vacuum cleaner wheels across the bare floors didn't surprise him. He'd heard her quick, light footsteps, the extra thunk of her heels on the wood. Ben looked around to see Annie dragging the industrial-size machine over to an outlet.

She was still in her red and black, her earrings merrily swinging to and fro as she stooped and jammed the plug into the wall socket. A long stretch of bare thigh ended in th small points of her knees.

"You were fast. You didn't have to come back." H wished she hadn't.

"Gabe was asleep on the floor with the kids. They're i bed, but when I shifted them, Gabe woke up and wandere down the hall. To bed, I think. He looked tired." The ribbe plastic tube of the cleaner ended at her shoulder when sh stood up and rested her shoe at the on-off switch of th vacuum. "I told him I'd help you."

"Not much to do. I'll finish. I usually wrap up down her and let Gabe call it a night." He took a stack of clean ash trays and placed the clear-glass, five-pointed receptacles o tables along one side of the room.

"Didn't your mother teach you that many hands mak light work?" Cheeky, she was, slouching with one hand o her hip, the other waggling the vacuum tube at him.

"No, Annie Conroy, my mother never taught me that." He lifted the trash bags and carried them to the door. He' take them out to the Dumpster before he shut down th lights and went up to bed.

"She should have." Interest and warmth sparked in he cloudy eyes. There was submerged curiosity there, too.

"I'm sure you're right." Ben covered the lemon and lim wedges, tipped the olives into a container and rejected An nie's sweetly offered interest.

Her curiosity about what he'd been taught or not taugh would have to remain unsatisfied.

Annie's curvy small body in her red cotton sweater an short black skirt was in motion again, her delicate frame quicksilver flash in the room as she hip-bumped chairs i front of her to one side.

The strength hidden by her slim, fine bones and pale ski caught him by surprise one more time. She looked fragile a hell, and he couldn't get over that contrast between silk an steel.

He wanted to test that combination, discover for himself how silk and steel moved with him, beneath him, in a yin yang of pleasure.

Wanting that discovery, wanting to see her smile bathing him with radiance in the moment when steel and silk became inexorably one, he shuddered and shifted uncomfortably.

His own curiosity would have to remain unsatisfied. His growing fascination for the sliver of light that was Annie Conroy unnerved him.

"Give me fifteen minutes with this monster machine, and after that I'm all yours." Her black shoe hovered over the vacuum switch.

Spoken without thought, her words bounced around among the images in his brain, spritzes of fire rising like sparks leaping in a dark sky.

"Yeah, well." Blood thick, rolling like a heavy tide through him, he shoved the wheeled bin of bottles and cans for recycling over to the storeroom. "Whatever." He couldn't talk through his suddenly dry mouth.

The idea of Annie Conroy all his for several hours slowed down his movements and turned his brain to oatmeal.

Her foot touched the vacuum cleaner.

For a moment, Ben didn't know if the roaring in his ears was his blood or the vacuum cleaner's rackety motor.

Annie's back-and-forth swoops over the floor, the metal machine trailing her, brought him back to reality. Released from the spell she'd heedlessly cast, Ben squirted cleaner on the grill. Disregarding the heavy thudding of his pulse, he scrubbed away at the last of the wispy images seducing him.

Gabe's angel was going to be the death of him.

An Indy 500 driver would have had a hard time keeping up with Annie on her turns around the room. Sweeping, swooping, shoving tables and chairs to one side, she moved through the room with an efficiency that was unlike her awkwardness around him.

Ben refused to contemplate the meaning of that knowledge.

By the time he'd cleaned out the grease from the grill and readied it for disposal, Annie had rolled the machine back into the storeroom and located the glass cleaner.

"Do you want me to help carry out the trash and bins after I clean the mirror and bottles on the shelf?" Standing near the jukebox, she'd tucked a roll of paper towels under her arm and was lugging a chair in the direction of the mirror behind the bar.

Looking up from the sludge of grease in the container, Ben banged the can down on the grill. "Damn it, Annie, go to bed."

Startled, she dropped the towels. "What?"

"It's eleven-thirty, you've been on your feet since God-knows-when and I want some time to myself." Glaring, he hefted the can and prepared to haul it outside.

"Oh." Helplessly, she glanced at the jar of cleaner in her hand and then at the towels on the floor.

"The Star's been rocking with people all night long. I like the quiet when everyone leaves. I like to finish the evening by myself. I like solitude." The pulsing beat of the music pounding through him made him more brutal than he'd intended.

Her face paled, and Ben saw the brightness vanish and the weariness she'd hidden all night behind her cheerful energy spread across her face. "Yes, I should have realized that's why Gabe went on to bed." She stooped slowly to pick up the towels. "Silly of me." Her movements stunned and slow, she placed the towels and cleaner on the bar. "You're right. I'll go to bed."

He fought the unexpected urge to offer comfort, to erase the quickly hidden hurt in her face. He might as well have shot Bambi for the way the look in her eyes made him feel, but he was glad she vanished quietly up the stairs to her bedroom, leaving behind her the lingering scent of her perfume and the pounding beat of the song.

Sagging against the bar with his outstretched arms bracing him, Ben let his head drop between the walls of his arms and let his conflicting emotions wash through him, need and desire and survival, a tidal wave threatening to crash over him and suck him out beyond the safety of the shore he'd claimed as his own for most of his life.

He spent a long time wiping down the jewel-toned liquor bottles, misting the mirror behind them and making it sparkle with the reflected liquids and bottle colors.

Alone in the shadowed room, going about his routine tasks, he found peace in the familiar, comfort of his own in the illusion of control over his life. It was a control he'd made his number one priority since he was eight years old, and he'd never lost sight of it since that day, no matter what events had followed. Control had become more important with each passing year, and he recognized that he was fighting that battle one more time. Only the weapons against him were soft and scented, warm, and all the more powerful for their softness, making him yearn for a woman who needed everything he wasn't.

He fought against the radiant weapons of Annie Conroy's sweetness and warmth, fought against that promise of something beyond his loneliness. He fought for his sake, and he fought for hers.

She didn't need a man like him in her life.

If he worried that his own survival depended on maintaining control, he knew damned well he'd destroy her.

All the bright warmth that seduced him would turn to chilly ashes, destroyed, under his influence.

And if, cleaning and polishing the interior of the Star, he wished that he were otherwise, well, life was what it was. A man had choices, and there was, if not relief, some satisfaction in making choices that had at least a tinge of honor to them.

On his way out the back door of the bar for the fifth time with the last of the trash for the Dumpster, Ben lifted a beer from the refrigerator and slipped it into the pocket of his slacks.

Listening to the cans clatter into their container, the bottles bang and smash against one another as they shattered into glistening bits of glass that caught the lights over the back door, Ben took a deep breath.

Warm and clean, a scent of earth and flowers swirling in the night, the air filled his lungs, stroked his skin.

Looking up at the cloudless, moonless sky, he paused. If he left the Star, he would miss these quiet evenings alone in the tropical nights.

He even liked the steamy summer nights when sweat dripped down his back with every trip to the Dumpster. Knowing he would miss the Star was, he knew, the best reason for making plans to leave. Because, unknowingly, unintentionally, he'd developed an attachment to his life here.

That knowledge had been nibbling at him since he'd told Annie that they should go *home, home* being the Star and whatever it had come to represent to him. Not a good sign, that slip. Four years in one place were obviously too long.

But then there was Gabe.

And Seagull.

Ben unscrewed the cap off his beer, flipped it into the trash, and strolled over to the stand of enormous oaks at the back of the bar's immediate area.

Strung between two of the largest oaks, the hammock was a good place to sit, sip a beer and think. He liked listening to the whisper of the night wind through the leaves of the old oaks and wondering how many other people over the years had heard the sighing of the leaves in the old trees.

With her black skirt and dark red top, she blended into the night. It was the darker shadow of her within the lighter ropes of the hammock that made him stop and look closer.

"Well, Annie Conroy, as I live and breathe. Seems like years since we've run into each other." He sighed. Inevitable. No matter what he did, no matter how he pushed, pushed, and pushed to keep her at a distance.

If there were a God, he must be having a good laugh.

Ben swallowed his beer.

So be it.

"Whoops." The hammock trembled and two long legs waved in his direction. "I don't think I can get out of this confounded spider's web. Seemed easy enough when I saw it, though."

"I thought you never slowed down."

"I was too keyed up to go to sleep after I checked on Will and Katie. They hadn't stirred since I put them to bed. They've had a tiring month." The hammock swung wildly and Annie grabbed the sides, hanging on. "Heavens. Maybe I should give up and roll out onto the ground." Swinging back and forth, the hammock confirmed her efforts. "I hate to give up, though."

"I've noticed." Ben tipped his beer and leaned against the oak supporting one end of the hammock. A lovely, lovely view of Annie stretched out with her hands to her side, her hair spread behind her head on the nonexistent pillow of the hammock ropes. With his foot, he set the hammock swinging again.

"Don't!" she gasped and swung one leg to the ground to drag the hammock to a stop. The hammock tilted toward the ground and wobbled.

"Josh was right, you know," Ben said casually, watching her scramble to maintain her balance. "A ride on the carousel has pleasures all its own." He inclined the hammock in the opposite direction. "Relax and look up at the sky, Annie. It's very peaceful out there, all that darkness. Forget about holding on. Relax and look up. And out."

"All right. I will." Determination and a certain be-damned-to-you attitude in her husky voice and the way she crossed her legs neatly at the ankles and held her arms to her sides. Resolution and tenacity in every tense line of her small frame.

"Uh, Annie," Ben said gently. "As I mentioned, the trick is to relax. There's no prize for effort."

"I don't want to fall." A squeak as she clutched the hammock.

For *fall,* Ben heard *fail.*

"You won't," he said. "I won't let you." He set the hammock moving with one hand. "Watch the sky, Annie. All that emptiness way out there, going on forever, emptiness."

For minutes on end, he inclined the hammock first one way, then the other.

And then she spoke, her voice muted and sad. "Is that what you see, Ben, when you look up at the sky? Darkness and emptiness?"

"That's what's there, Annie Conroy. Nothing more." Draining the last of his beer, Ben propped it on the soft ground under the oak and went to stand at the side of the hammock. He sank carefully onto the edge of the hammock. "No, don't try to sit up," he said as she stirred uneasily. "You're not going to tip over." He leaned across her knees and rested his hand on the far edge, balancing their weights. "What do you see, Angel-Annie?"

"What?" She moved restlessly.

"When you look up at all that darkness, what do you see?" He slipped off one small leather shoe and took her slim foot in his hand. He'd known her foot would feel this way, narrow, arching, the toes delicate punctuation points at the end of the high arch.

She was quiet, only the flexing of her fingers against the hammock moving as he rubbed the sole of her foot, massaging his thumb into the spot under her toes.

"Come on, Annie," he encouraged, not clear for the moment what he was encouraging her to do as he ran his thumb under her arch and felt her toes curl toward him.

"Look up there, Ben." She raised her arm and pointed between the canopy of oak branches and leaves. "See that star? The brightest one?"

He nodded and stroked the top of her foot with his index finger.

"I look at that star and I feel wonder." She pointed to another, less-bright star. "All those ancient fires burning way out there in space, their light falling on us."

"Those worlds are dead, Annie. Fires long-gone in some cases. Nothing there except a light from a dead star."

"I know. But I don't see emptiness, Ben. I look and see the wonder of life shining like a beacon from the past, showing us the way."

"The way to nothing, Annie," he murmured, enclosing her foot in his hand. "If it's a beacon, it's a beacon to nowhere."

"Maybe." She paused, and then continued, her voice soft and filled with the wonder she was describing. "But I look up there at all those stars, the planets, and I think of how much I don't know about everything, the wonder behind all the things I don't understand." She shifted so that she was looking in another direction. "Wouldn't you like to be able to soar among those stars, Ben, and know, really *know* the secrets of the universe?"

"Nope." And he wouldn't. He had no curiosity about that empty sky. "Trying to figure out what I'm going to do each day is enough for me." He slipped off her other shoe and smoothed his palm over it. Nobody would have any trouble convincing him, though, that Annie's foot *was* a miracle of nature, he thought as he worked his fingers between her toes and wiggled them. He wondered absently if he were developing a foot fetish as he bent her toes forward, loosening the tightness he sensed in the ball of her foot. "To tell you the truth, Annie, I don't have a whole lot of curiosity about much except what I see in front of me."

"But who would have ever thought a hundred years ago that the dust of the moon would show man's footprints?" She swung her arm in a circle. "A hundred years from now, who knows what someone looking up at the sky will see?" She tilted her chin heavenward and her hair fell over the side of the hammock as she glanced north.

"I'm curious about you, Annie." So sleek, that skin over all those tiny bones. Twenty-two of them, he recalled from seventh grade health class.

He recalled other things from seventh grade hygiene, too, and he chuckled.

"What's so funny?" She lifted her head.

"Oh, I remembered our seventh grade teacher trying to explain the difference between male and female reproduction without ever mentioning sex. We were a confused bunch of hormones for a month or two. Until we got everything figured out satisfactorily."

"Oh, *sex,*" she muttered scornfully. "That's no big deal," she said, waving her arm dismissively.

"Oh, yes, Annie, it's a *very* big deal," he said and leaned over her, his large shadow falling across her as he took her mouth with his and kissed her, falling into darkness.

A soft sigh, hers. A muffled groan, his. The whole universe shrunken to the gleam of her pale face between his hands, his harsh breathing, the wonder of Annie Conroy soft beneath him and kissing him back.

Chapter Eight

If she'd thought the heavens held wonder, it was nothing to the wonder of Ben Jackson's mouth over hers urging her into a glittering universe where anything was possible, where everything was touch and taste, where the slide of his tongue over her lips was a dark and dangerous taste, and she opened to that skillful touch, to the wonder he created between them with the skim of his hand over her breast.

She clung to the sides of the swaying hammock, the scratchy roughness of its rope against her palms the sole reality in all the burning, her anchor to a world that seemed pastel next to the glowing red and gold he offered her with each stroke of his tongue, each slow stroke of his hand against her bare skin.

His was a man's skill, a man's urgency, and he took her fast and far to a place she'd never imagined. A place where she lost the defining edge of herself as he settled over her, his broad chest a welcome weight against the ache in her breasts, a weight she wanted closer. She lifted against him, straining to erase the last space between them.

"Easy, angel," he murmured, his breath shivering against her ear. His muscular thighs slid between her legs and he rocked once, convulsively, and she was shivering endlessly with the weight of him lying against her, the hammock swaying underneath.

She'd never imagined that the touch of a man's mouth moving over the slope of her neck could make her ache, *ache,* and she turned her neck to his hungry mouth, tipping her chin and inviting the skim of that heat lower.

But it was the back of his hand that slid over her neck, nudged the neckline of her sweater to one side and lingered, his knuckles burning across her skin at the neckline of her sweater. The tip of one finger under the cotton was so close to the aching inside her that she forgot to breathe, wanting that stroking, heated touch against her nipple.

Clinging to the sides of the hammock, she raised her knee, anchoring herself to him in the swaying, rocking darkness. "Please," she whispered. "Please."

"Anything that pleases you, angel, everything." Rough, rough like the hammock rope, his callused hand eased her skirt back. "Sweet, sweet Annie. Let me..." And his hand smoothed over her knee, behind the bend.

Dazed, her eyelids heavy, Annie opened her eyes and saw the stars, distant and sparkling, a promise in the darkness of the vast sky, and clenching the hammock, she turned her mouth once more to his, her lips soft and yielding to the hard hunger of his seeking lips and tongue, answering him, telling him of her own need in quiet, hushed sighs that slipped away into the night.

The need to touch him drew her hands up and around his neck. His hair was slippery-soft under her fingers, beguiling her. The ridge of muscles across the back of his shoulders was strong, flexing to her touch, and all the while he kissed her deeply, smashing her defenses with a desperate hunger.

Even dazed she sensed his desperation, knew the loneliness driving him, and she longed to give him refuge from the darkness she felt in him, wanted him to see the stars gleaming above them, wanted him to know in these moments before the dawn of Christmas Eve day that there was more than bleakness and desolation.

One warm palm slid around her neck and his fingers stroked the lobe of her ear, tugging at it until tremors rolled through her and she held him tightly, letting the tremors roll like the sweep of a mighty river in flood tide from her into him, and she kissed him back, again and again, letting her touch speak to him of joy and hope, of the possibility of happiness, whispering to him with her touch to look up, look up at the brightness shining above them.

And then the world was spinning around her, darkness and stars, the oak canopy and the hard ground, and she was sprawled over Ben, cradled between his thighs, the hammock pitching above them.

One arm tightened over her hips, binding her to him, and, running his hand up her spine, he cupped the nape of her neck and drew her face down to his. His fingers tangled in the mass of her hair falling over him and his kiss turned into something else, a kiss suddenly so dark and fierce that control trembled at the abyss, the reins abandoned.

Or lost.

"You're the wonder, Annie Conroy," he muttered, outlining the edge of her ear with his finger. "What are you doing to me?" And he rose to a half-sitting position, rocking her back and forth in the chair of himself. "What am I doing to you?" He laid his chin on top of her head and rocked again, his movement dying and ending with both of them sitting up and his arms around her, his chin still resting on her head, his warm breath stirring the strands of her hair.

Her knees were somewhere in the vicinity of his armpits, her arms around his chest, and she opened her eyes. The thick column of his neck was all she saw, but as he raised his head and moved back, she lifted her face to his.

The muscles of his hard-angled face were pulled tight, his expression caught between pleasure and pain. Annie touched his jawline, following the bunched muscle there that spoke of control gained at the last moment.

"I know what I was doing, Ben," she murmured, smoothing and touching the knotted muscles of his face until she felt him relax and he finally looked at her.

"Think so?" Amusement hovered in his lazy syllables. "I doubt it. Angel-Annie, you don't strike me as someone who's carrying a world-class load of experience around on your shoulders." Slowly, regretfully, he tiptoed his fingers down the vertebrae of her spine, one by one, until he clasped her hips and lifted her off his lap.

"It was only a kiss." She smoothed her skirt down, flattening the wrinkles out.

"Since the minute you walked into the Star, I've wondered what it would be like to kiss you, Angel-Annie, *really* kiss you. Believe me," he said, looking up at her, "this was something outside my experience."

Standing over him, Annie reached out her hand. "Whatever it was, I don't regret it."

"I do," he muttered, rising in one quick flex of muscled thighs. "And you should." Grasping her shoulders, he leaned down to her. "Don't you understand? I was this close—" he snapped his thumb and finger together "—to forgetting who I was, who you are, to forgetting you have two children asleep upstairs over my bar." He dropped his hands and waited while his chest rose twice. "Annie, I almost lost control. I don't lose control with women. Ever."

He walked over and plucked her shoes from their resting place on the sandy, weedy ground. Clunking the heels together, he emptied the shoes of sand and handed them to her.

"Thanks." Annie stepped into her shoes. She wanted to tell him that he was wrong, she *had* known exactly what she was doing, but she knew he wouldn't believe her. He'd made up his mind that he was the instigator, she the maiden whose experience didn't qualify her to resist his blandishments.

That was the trouble with fair-maiden myths. Nobody ever believed that the fair maiden knew exactly what she wanted and had a right to ask for it. She'd known very well that she wanted his kisses, his touch. She'd wanted to return his kisses. Anger tingled in her fingertips, and she knew a momentary impulse to punch him on his square jaw as she watched him struggle for words and control. If she took a tiny bit of delight in the fact that his effort didn't come easily, she forgave herself.

Her foot tapping the sandy ground, Annie recognized the moment when his control was firmly back in his grasp.

Ben slipped one hand inside his slacks pocket, his stance entirely too casual to be completely convincing, and, with his other hand, he pushed the hammock slowly, watching her as he spoke. "Careless sex is the surest road to disaster. I let the situation get out of control, Annie. And I'm not a disaster junkie."

"Excuse me. Do you have a piece of paper and a pen? Or pencil?"

"A pen?" Ben dropped the metal loop at the end of the hammock rope cords.

Patting her pockets, Annie continued, "Because I'd like to take notes. I might want to use your lecture with Will or Katie."

"I'm sorry." Both hands jammed deeply into his pockets now, he shrugged. "I didn't mean to hurt your feelings."

"Oh, you didn't." Piqued by his determination to assume control over the issue of fault, she walked over to him until he had to look at her. "You might ask yourself, though, why you're arrogantly leaping over the fact that perhaps *I* could have called a halt to our *mutual* kiss even though you're a terrific kisser."

He shrugged again, unconvinced.

"I kissed you back, you know, and with great pleasure, I might add, but that was *all* that happened. A kiss." Annie tapped his chest. "And, although you might not believe this, I am *not* a person who engages in *careless* or *casual* sex. A woman with two children doesn't have time—or energy—for careless or casual. Not usually," she tacked on, outrage giving way to fairness.

"I've insulted you." His hands were doubled into fists in his pockets.

"Yes. I believe you have."

"I'm sorry." He frowned. "I never thought you were that kind of woman."

"*Sorry* doesn't butter the bread," she said as she marched steadily toward the light at the back door. "Or didn't your mother teach you that, either?"

"Annie, I don't even know what that means." He kept pace with her, one long stride to two of hers.

Darn man. She would have forgiven him if he'd been able to keep the laughter out of his voice. She whirled and grabbed the placket of his shirt. "It means, you self-important, tunnel-visioned male, that actions speak louder than words. Apologizing doesn't get you off the hook." She whipped around and opened the door and stepped into the storeroom. "Even if it is almost Christmas."

All the way up the stairs, she knew he didn't take his gaze off her, and she resisted the urge to turn around and stick out her tongue. So there, Ben Jackson. Put that in your pipe and smoke it, she thought with exhilaration as she went into her sleeping children.

Ben heard Annie close the bedroom door extremely carefully, a world of meaning in her *careful* shutting of the door. He had hurt her. The indignation bristling in her small body as she'd read him the riot act had been real.

If he were honest, he'd have to admit he deserved every pointed accusation. It had been arrogant of him to assume that she didn't know her own mind. But he still blamed himself for letting the kiss get out of hand. She didn't know how close he'd come to slipping that soft red sweater down to her waist, past her slim hips and off, how close he'd come to sliding her next-to-nonexistent black skirt up to her waist and making love— Ben stopped.

It wouldn't have been making love. That was why he'd tried to apologize. Annie didn't deserve what he was offering. And what he was offering wasn't much, for damned sure. He'd reminded himself all night long that he wasn't good for her, reminded himself that she didn't need a man like him around, but the first chance he'd had, he'd proved himself right.

Listening to the sounds of her shoes hitting the floor, the squeaking of the bedsprings, Ben admitted to himself that he wouldn't have stopped if they hadn't tumbled out of the hammock and onto the damp ground. She'd been through too much during the last few days, and he'd caught her at a vulnerable moment, played on her need for comfort and, despite her accusation of arrogance, he knew her experience was nowhere in his league.

But she might have stopped him.

If she hadn't, she wouldn't have forgiven herself in the morning.

And he would never have forgiven himself for using her.

He didn't want to remember that he almost hadn't stopped.

Making the rounds of the bar and turning off the last of the lights and setting the burglar alarm, he tried to forget that Annie was upstairs.

Later, showered and lying awake in his bed, watching the shadows grow lighter as morning approached, Ben heard the restless turning of Gabe down the hall, the sleepy murmur of Katie during the night, the creaking of the old boards, and he was piercingly aware of the people around him, his responsibility for them.

He wanted to throw on his clothes and hightail it down the highway.

In the morning when he looked at the tables in the Star, he wished he'd had enough gumption to leave while he could.

"Gabe?" Caught in a nightmare, Ben shook his head. "What the hell's going on?"

Straightening up from behind the bar with a carton of eggs in her hands, Annie glanced at him and then quickly away, busying herself with cracking eggs into a skillet and buttering pieces of toast as they popped up from the eight-slice toaster.

From the table nearest the stairs, Katie twinkled up at him. "We dec'rated. Me and Will did. Early. Mr. Gabe helped."

Every table in the room sprouted green gherkin Christmas trees.

Katie and Will had stuck toothpicks into each gherkin, fashioning evergreen trees. For the lower branches, they'd toothpicked three gherkins together. For the trunks of the trees, they'd used the big dill pickles, slashing off the bottoms for stability. A green-ruffled cocktail toothpick topped off each tree with a final flourish and a white paper napkin hid the base of the trees.

Looking at the strange creations, Ben didn't want to know what Katie had used to keep the trees upright.

"I told the kiddies they could decorate," Gabe said, facing him like a bantam rooster. "We need a little holiday spirit around this joint."

Unable to look away from the forest, Ben wondered if maybe he'd gone sleepwalking in the night and downed a pint of bourbon.

"Katie, I told you *he* wouldn't like 'em," Will said and scooted away. "I *knew* it was a baby idea."

Trudging over to Ben, her rag doll dangling from one hand, Katie pulled at the crease of his slacks. "You do so like our cheerful trees, don't you, Mr. Ben?"

Awaiting the death verdict, Will had retreated to a corner of the room where he shoved one cheerful tree around and around the table.

"I don't like decorations. Christmas or otherwise," Ben croaked, stunned into immobility by the solution to the mystery of the disappearing gherkins.

"But these are special. You will like these," Katie stated with utter confidence, but not releasing him.

"Maybe."

"We made them for you. You have to see them up close." She tugged.

Ben surrendered to the childish certainty and walked over to a table.

"See?" Katie touched the ruffled loops of the cocktail toothpick. "S-o-o-o pretty," she crooned, pressing the shiny plastic and lifting her doll to see.

"Won't they rot?"

"Not by tomorrow," Gabe snapped. "Shut up and enjoy the festivities. Hell's bells. They're damned Christmas trees. In miniature."

"A whole jar of gherkins is what's sitting in front of me." Ben could smell the pickles.

"It'll be easier if you don't think of them as your gherkins, old son," Gabe advised. "They'll grow on you the longer you look at them." His chortle was at Ben's expense.

So were the gherkins.

"I know, I know," Gabe consoled, reading his mind, "but as for the gherkins, hell, I'll chip in for them. I can afford a damned bottle of gherkins for Christmas, I reckon." He shuffled over to Will, saying something Ben couldn't hear, but Will's covert squint at Ben and shake of the head weren't reassuring.

"You will hang our red bows, too, on your real tree," Katie ordered, Ben's surrender having established her rights. "But you got to find a little tree. We lost some of our bows, you see, but we are happy to share." She leaned confidingly against his leg. "Sharing is part of Kissmus, you know."

"Uh, Katie, I have to go to work." Ben looked down at the urchin peeking up at him, her dishwater-brown hair straggling around her small, plain face.

Scrutinizing his face, she nodded. "I know. You got things to do. Mommy said to stay out of the way. Will and me got work to do, too. Kissmus p'sents. I will make you sum'pin extra special," she said as she hippety-hopped in the direction of her brother.

Ben groaned, the sound welling up from the lowest depths. Decorations. Presents. He was going down for the count.

"Breakfast. Come and get it, troops," Annie sang out, her voice as cheerful as the damned gherkin trees.

Choosing to eat at the bar while the troops gathered around a table with its sugar-vinegary-smelling centerpiece, Ben ate quickly, rinsed his dishes, stacked them in the dishwasher and headed for the back door.

He refused to participate in the search that Gabe was organizing for a "Kissmus" tree.

Staying out of everyone's way during the long, interminable day required every ounce of Ben's ingenuity.

He'd turn a corner and run into Annie. They'd both back off so fast that it was surprising one of them didn't trip and break a leg, Ben reckoned as he bumped into her for the fifth time in an hour. "Sorry." He rubbed his hands over his hair. "I mean—oh, hell with it." He left.

Every time he saw Katie, she giggled and smiled at him. Will, on the alert, stayed two steps ahead of Ben all day, the

oy's skinny behind vanishing around a door frame or up
he stairs as Ben approached.

"Them kiddies are not in the way," Gabe insisted as he
aw Ben scowling after Will.

"Hell they aren't." He flapped the towel against the
toreroom door frame. "No. It's not the kids, Gabe. You
now that." He walked into the storeroom to finish the in-
entory he'd started two days earlier. "If you like all the
henanigans, I reckon I can put up with some holiday spirit
or this year, at least."

"I knew you could. You're not as cold as you pretend."

"In fact, I'm worse, but you and your cherubs and An-
el-Annie have me outnumbered. I figured I had two
hoices. Take off for the next few days, or endure."

"Why'd you decide to stick around, old son?" Gabe slit
pen a box and began racking rows of mustard onto a board
helf.

"I'm not sure." Ben looked up from the row of tally
narks. "Although to tell you the truth, once or twice I
ooked at my ankles to see if somehow during the night
omeone had welded a ball and chain and shackled me to a
vall in the Star."

"Can't always see chains."

"Oh, here we go. Wisdom from the ancient one," Ben
aid and laughed. "I'll get through it, Gabe, but don't think
his changes anything, not in the long run." Ben saw the
lick of Annie's purple dress pass the corner of the store-
oom door as he went on slowly, choosing his words care-
ully. He hadn't planned on bringing up the conclusion he'd
eached, but one time was no better than another. "In fact,
Jabe, I've been turning over the idea that it's about time for
ne to head down the long road again."

Gabe's gnarled hands knocked over a pepper can. "Why
on't we put that idea on hold, Ben? Get back to it after tax
ime. We shouldn't make any major decisions right now.

Later. We'll see about this cockamamy idea later." He stacked the pepper on top of a row of silver-and-red cans.

Annie's purple dress flashed at the edge of Ben's vision again and he lost his train of thought for the moment.

Maybe Gabe was right. They would thrash out the idea later.

The Star was empty by eight-thirty that evening, most of the customers headed for home and Christmas Eve. Staring at the empty room where Annie cleared tables with hummingbird speed, Ben wondered what he would do for the rest of the evening. He had no intention of running into Annie in some secluded corner of the bar or outside in the privacy of the cool dark night.

So he stayed downstairs, making jobs for himself, cleaning out the refrigerator, pitching out perfectly good slabs of butter and margarine, dumping a partially empty cardboard cylinder of vanilla ice cream he'd used for some creamy drink a week earlier.

As a rule, the Star's clientele steered away from fancy drinks, apparently convinced that the bar's rustic nature called for basic down-home beer and whiskey.

Spreading out a stack of papers in front of him, he finished the inventory paperwork and began running through the columns of numbers to see how the accounts balanced for the month.

The creak of the bar stool alerted him, and he looked up from the table where he'd spread his papers to see Katie perched on the stool.

"Hi, Mr. Ben," she said in her soft lisp. "You're busy. I'm jes' sittin' here. Please ignore me." She folded her hands on top of her doll resting on the bar.

Ben punched out the numbers on his calculator, the long strip of paper curling in loops in front of him.

Not possible to ignore a child who sat so absolutely still, not talking, only watching his every movement. Ben looked over at her. "Does your mom know you're down here?"

Katie shook her head, her dark blue eyes big and solemn. "She's helping Gabe change his sheets and scrub the bathroom. Gabe is tired and Mommy didn't want him to do anything else for the day."

Alert, Ben put down his pencil "Is Gabe all right?"

Nodding, Katie popped her thumb in her mouth. "He said his bones are telling him the weather." The almost invisible line of her eyebrows met above her nose. "Is Mr. Gabe going to be sick like my gramma?"

Tapping his pencil on the calculator, Ben searched Katie's dark eyes before answering. "Gabe hasn't broken any bones. He works hard, so he gets tired after busy days. Sometimes he can tell the weather's going to change because his bones hurt. That's all he meant." Ben took his glasses off and folded them on top of the papers.

Whirling once around on the stool, Katie grabbed the bar edge and stopped herself. "I like your glasses, Mr. Ben."

"Thank you, Katie." How did you talk with a five-year-old? Off in one direction, then another. "But you haven't told me who knows where you've gone. Your mom will worry if she doesn't know where you are, won't she?"

Her pause was too long.

"No one will worry?"

Most parents would. If he were a father, he'd worry all the time. How did parents ever sleep through the night? He stood up and walked around the bar to the service side, stopping where she twirled on the stool.

"Come on, Katie. Who knows where you are?"

"Will's in charge of me. I told him I had Kissmus errands and I would be back soon." Katie stood up on the rung of the bar stool and leaned toward him. Her wispy hair fluttered like a halo around her, the no-color brown momentarily catching the light and shining like corn tassels. "Will is afraid of you, Mr. Ben. He says you don't like us."

"That so?" Ben was surprised by the twinge of hurt. He'd known the kid was leery of him, so why should Katie's announcement come as any big shock? "I like you."

Nodding earnestly, Katie said, "I told him he was wrong. I told him you had sad eyes." She peered closely and nodded. "I was right."

"Tell you what, Katie Conroy," Ben said as he lifted a beer out of the refrigerator. "Run upstairs and tell your mom you're having a cola with me, okay?"

"Can't." Her small mouth flipped wrong side up. She looked as if he'd asked her to climb Mount Vesuvius.

Ben paused. Katie's flights of conversation were beginning to have an intriguing logic. He could almost figure out where she was headed. "Why can't you?"

"No cola at night." She looked over her shoulder as she confessed, "I might not wake up in the night. *You* know, *before.*" She rolled her eyes. "And I'm way too old for not waking up even if Will says I'm only a baby."

"I see." And Ben did. He hadn't thought of that childish fear for twenty-eight years, not since he was four, but suddenly, there it was, intense and humiliating, and he didn't want Katie embarrassed. "Milk, then. But go tell her where you are, Katie."

As she twirled on the stool, her barrette slid down a strand of hair and clattered onto the bar. "I like milk. With five cherries in it. Mr. Gabe fixed cherry milk last night." She clearly assumed that Ben would be able to produce the same culinary delight. Handing him the barrette, Katie said, "Please squoosh it into my hair so it does not hang into my eyes."

Ben glanced from the barrette to her, bewildered by the request. Why didn't she take the barrette upstairs to her mother? "I don't know how to fix little girls' hair, Katie."

"You will do very well." Trustingly, she leaned her head forward, the hair, as predicted, straggling into her eyes.

"All right. I'll try." Turning the barrette over and over in his hands, Ben studied the blue plastic bar with its wing-to-wing angels along the top. It should function like a paper clip. Or a spring clip. Twiddling the metal prongs, he undid the barrette and lifted Katie's hank of hair, scooping it back and off her thin face and clipping the plastic bar in place.

The barrette stayed for a second before clattering back onto the bar. Katie's hair drooped into her eyes again.

"I am having a *very* bad hair day," she said glumly, brushing her hair free of her eyes.

"What?" Ben stared at her.

She nodded. "I have many bad hair days." Her small face became sad as her gaze lingered on the swish-swish of the hula doll's skirts. Ben tussled the barrette into a locked, secure position in Katie's fine, slippery hair. "She's pretty," Katie said, acceptance heavy in her baby-lisp. "I am not."

Ben snapped the prongs of Katie's barrette around a larger clump of hair. The bar was lopsided, one end sticking skyward, the other lying close to her narrow head, but the barrette seemed secure. He glanced at the hula doll and back to Katie's wistful face as she stared at the cheap toy.

The tiny lights around the doll's skirt reflected into the mirror and back, turning the garish plastic skirt into a shimmering magic of moving color, and shining onto Katie's plain face with its too-big eyes and stringy hair.

Ben frowned. He wanted to reassure the small female inside the child and didn't have the faintest idea what to say.

At his frown, Katie patted his cheek. "'s okay. Mommy says I've got sum'pin better. She says I've got character and good bones. And they'll last a lifetime," she said earnestly, tilting her thin face to Ben.

Examining her face carefully, unbearably touched by Katie's hope that good bones and character would see her over life's rough patches, Ben touched her small nose. "Your mom's right, kid. You've got *great* bones. All the really terrific-looking women do. And, Katie," Ben said seriously, "I should know. I've seen gorgeous women in China. In Iceland. *Everywhere*," he assured her. "And great bones are the secret, believe me." Watching her weigh what he'd said, Ben couldn't believe he'd been so extravagant with his words.

Not like him at all.

Then Katie's impish smile flashed across her plain face, transforming it, and in that smile, Ben saw a promise of the woman she would become in a few years, entrancing, delightful and with character to spare.

Plain little Katie was right. She had something better than pretty.

But she gazed again at the hula doll and a tiny sigh escaped. "She's like a fairy princess, isn't she, Mr. Ben?"

Leaning over the bar, Ben lowered his voice. "But take it from me, kid. She doesn't have great bones. As for her character, well, I couldn't say."

Katie's dark eyes were a mystery of miniature femininity as she nodded with absolute certainty. "I know. Because you're a gentleman."

Ben blinked. "A gentleman?" he said, trying not to roar with laughter. If little Katie only knew. He'd never been promiscuous, and especially not in his later years, but he'd been a very curious male in his younger days.

"Of course. Gentlemen don't discuss ladies."

"Another lesson from your mom?" He covered his mouth and coughed, turning his head so Katie wouldn't see his grin.

"Mr. Gabe." She slid off the stool, her jeans-clad legs scissoring her to the floor.

"Yeah. I might have figured." Ben reached into the refrigerator and took out the milk carton. "Go tell your mom where you are, Katie."

But Katie didn't have to.

Annie had stepped around the door frame as Katie bumped to the floor. "Go on to bed, Katie Sue. I'll bring your milk up."

"Want my cherry milk with Mr. Ben." Katie faced her mother. "We was talking. And I have Kissmus errands. I forgot to ask Mr. Ben about my errand." She wrinkled her face.

Stooping, Annie placed her hands on her daughter's shoulders. "What do you need, Katie?"

"I need 'lumnum. Foil. For p'sents."

Rummaging under the bar, Ben handed Annie a box of aluminum foil. Her cool fingertips brushed his, and she shot him a bemused look from under her spiky gold eyelashes.

"Upstairs, punkin. Now." Annie took Katie's shoulders and reversed the child's direction, heading her to the stairs.

When the little girl had vanished, Annie stayed, her hands clasped in front of her. In her red sweater and black skirt, she was a dramatic streak of color and contrast in the uncertain light of the room.

She cleared her throat. "Thank you, Ben."

After their intimacy in the hammock, they'd both been wary of each other. He'd thought they'd skate around each other for the next week, both edgy and on guard. Whatever he'd expected her to say, it wasn't "thanks."

"For what?" He hooked his hands under his arms and observed her fidgeting.

She cleared her throat again and shifted position. She reminded him of her son and his to-and-fro leg-hopping. Annie Conroy was in an apologizing mode. And she was uncomfortable.

"For what you said. To Katie. You were wonderful with her. I owe you."

"You don't owe me anything, Annie. I don't want your gratitude." And he didn't.

"What do you want, Ben Jackson?" she whispered, shifting her black-shod feet. "Do you know?"

His laugh was ironic. "I sure don't. And that's the joker in the whole cotton-picking pack of cards. I don't know what in hell I want. From life. From the Star. From you. But I know damned well it's not your gratitude, I want, Angel-Annie."

"All right." Too much sympathy in her sweet face, too much understanding. "But I won't forget the gift you just gave Katie. She'll never look in the mirror and see herself as plain little Katie Conroy after what you told her."

"It was the truth."

Annie walked over to him behind the bar and stood on tiptoe. Touching his cheek with her soft, cool lips, she whispered, "Merry Christmas, Ben Jackson."

After she'd left, Ben stared for a long time at the twitching, flashing lights on the hula doll before he gathered up his papers and turned off all the lights except for the ones on the hula doll.

As he went upstairs, he glanced through the stained-glass window down at the bar. In the darkness, the twinkling lights of the hula doll glowed beneath him.

Chapter Nine

Katie woke Annie up with pats on her cheek. "Mommy! Mommy! Santa Claus!"

Annie opened one bleary eye to her daughter's fresh-faced innocence. After the children had finally gone to sleep, she'd stayed up. Like Katie, she had Kissmus errands.

"Go back to sleep, Katie. I told you Santa Claus wouldn't find us way out here," Will grumbled.

"I heard the bells, and I went downstairs. I saw!" whispered Katie, excitement shivering her all over. "I bet Mr. Josh is Santa Claus, Will. I bet, I bet!" She wiggled over Annie, crawling over the sheets and blanket to Will, her heels bumping Annie's chin.

"*Oomph*, puddin-head. Watch those lethal weapons." Annie struggled to a sitting position through a clump of wriggling, squirming children.

"Katie's wrong. Right, Mommy?" Even Will's chin was quivering with excitement. From the elevated heights of seven, he *knew* Katie was wrong, but an element of doubt had him shaking, too.

"I think she imagined she heard Santa Claus, Will. Anyway, we forgot to put out the milk, and we forgot to leave him a letter. He'll catch up with us next year." Annie rubbed her face and looked at her watch. Seven in the morning. Maybe she was lucky Katie hadn't dreamed bells at six a.m.

"That's what I said." Will nodded, the excitement draining from him.

"P'sents, p'sents. And a tree! Without dec'rations! Come see!" Katie sang, dragging the sheets and blanket off Annie and Will, and running to the door, throwing it open.

"Gabe's making pancakes." Ben's fist was raised to knock.

Annie's green T-shirt with the reindeer prancing across it was rumpled around her bottom and the sheets were a jumble on the floor as she stared into Ben Jackson's face.

Her stomach fluttered when she saw the glint in his hazel eyes as he took in the whole of her sleep-rumpled self, her legs sprawled every-which-way, her face creased with pillow marks.

Frozen in place by the look on his face, she watched the shutters drop, but she recognized what she saw in the strained white lines around his mouth.

Pulling at her T-shirt, grabbing the sheets back onto the bed, Annie panicked and dived off the bed onto the far side, landing on her fanny.

"Shut the door, Katie." Ben's voice was harsh, echoing in Annie's ears, a rough caress, even after she heard his footsteps going down the stairs.

"Oh, Katie, now you've done it," Will said, anxiety back in his stiff body.

"Have not. Come see, Will," Katie crooned as she pulled out a red T-shirt from a suitcase and worked herself into her jeans.

"Uh, guys, hold on a minute. Let me get dressed. We'll all go down together. Go wash your faces and brush your teeth while I get dressed and make up the bed. Don't go downstairs without me." Annie wanted the barricade of her children around her before she faced Ben again.

Astonished by the brief moment when he'd stood at the doorway, she still couldn't believe her reaction. She'd never in her life turned to melted butter when a man looked at her. This was not a good time to change her habits. Especially not with a man like Ben Jackson.

She yawned and twisted her head from side to side. Katie and Will were restless sleepers, and they took up most of the bed space, spending their sleep-time roaming from the foot of the bed back to the headboard. She felt as though she'd slept in a blender.

"I mean it. Wait for me." She handed them their toothbrushes. "And I have to brush your hair, Katie."

Katie's shoeless feet thumped against the bare floorboards as she ran down the hall, but Will followed more slowly. With Katie wound up and flying off the wall, Annie knew time was short. She threw on her clothes, snapped the sheets and blanket into the air and settled them quickly over the bed, tucking in the corners as Katie and Will poked their heads around the edge of the door.

"You're not ready," Katie wailed. "Hurry, hurry!"

"I am, Katie. The only thing moving faster than I am right now is a whirlwind," Annie muttered, sinking onto the bed and drawing Katie backward between her knees as she braided Katie's hair and worked leftover red ribbon into the skimpy braid. "There you are, sugarplum."

Katie peeped into the mirror, twisting her head so she could admire the ribbon threaded into her braid. "Pretty Kissmus ribbon."

"Give me three minutes in the bathroom and we'll go downstairs and sample Gabe's pancakes." Annie raced fulltilt out the door and down the hall.

She could smell the bacon and pancakes from the head of the stairs. Gabe was definitely making breakfast, and, somehow, the homely food smells reminded her of Christmases past and the way she'd always waited for her parents before going downstairs to see the presents under the tree.

A year after she'd married Larry, her parents had traveled to Africa for the trip they'd been saving up for all their lives. They'd made a bad choice of tour guides. The rhinoceros that had tipped over their Range Rover and killed them had been hungry, thirsty and enraged.

Annie had saved the picture they'd sent her from Africa. Taken as they'd departed for what would become their final trek, they were dressed in bush clothes, their arms linked around each other. Even under the brims of their helmets, she'd seen that they were laughing. Sitting up nursing Will, his sweaty little forehead bumping at her one night during the worst of her grief and loneliness, she'd thought the pain would never leave. Unable to stop her muffled sobs and the rain of tears that dripped onto Will, she'd taken out a magnifying glass and pored over that fading picture. Seeing their blissful grins, she'd never again regretted their decision to go a-roaming. Though she'd cried, though she still missed them, she'd known they'd been happy. And she'd finally known peace.

Smelling Gabe's bacon now, Annie remembered all that old happiness, and some of Katie's excitement rippled through her as she held Will's and Katie's hands tightly to her and went downstairs.

There wouldn't be a Christmas tree. Of course not. There wouldn't be presents. She'd already told the children that their Christmas would be sharing the day with one another. She knew all that, didn't expect anything else, but still—

"Oh, my," she said as she entered the room.

Gabe's back was to her and he had a stack of dollar-size pancakes on a big platter. Ben had one fist around a short pine tree jammed into a cola can. Next to the tree, two packages in wrinkled newspaper waited, Katie's name on one in red marker, Will's on the other.

Her red bows lay spread out on the bar.

"Oh, my," she repeated, unable to make sense of what she saw.

"Told you there were p'sents."

If Ben had said anything, Annie thought she might sit right down on the floor and bawl.

With the children by her side, she walked over to Gabe and hugged him around his skinny waist. Knowing her smile trembled, she looked at Ben.

"Sit down, kiddos. I made one tree-shaped and one star-shaped pancake for each of you." Gabe motioned to one of the tables. "The rest of us have to make do with dull old circles. Let's eat." He plopped the platter onto the table and sat down with them. "Ben? You going to stand there like a fool, or are you going to eat?"

Ben sat. The tree didn't fall. And Annie couldn't stop smiling.

"Told Ben we were going to have a tree. You kiddos can decorate it after breakfast."

Syrup smeared around his mouth, Will tried to ignore the tree and the packages, but Annie saw his gaze return again and again to the tree propped on top of the gleaming wood of the bar.

"Mr. Gabe?" Katie pulled off a piece of pancake and nibbled it. Katie didn't like syrup and ate her pancakes dry. "Are the p'sents from Santa?"

Gabe scratched his balding head. "Nope. From me and Ben."

Annie didn't believe a word Gabe said. She seriously doubted that Ben had had much to do with the lumpily wrapped presents and the Leaning-Tower-of-Pisa tree.

"That's okay." Katie said. "We have p'sents for you and Ben. When do you want them?"

Ben's knife clattered against his plate, but he didn't say anything.

"Um, Katie," Annie said, thinking quickly, "you can give Ben and Gabe their presents later in the day. After

Christmas dinner?'' Silently she checked with Gabe, who nodded. ''That way you and Will can decorate the tree.''

His craggy face expressionless, Ben was a silent presence at the table. There, but on the outside of their shared circle of happiness, a nonparticipant.

And so he stayed throughout the day.

Will shaped a foil angel and folded it around the top of the tree. Katie took garbage bag twists and slipped them through the loops of the red bows, tying the bows to the tree. Perched on the bar, she followed a decorating scheme only she could figure out, and the finished product had an abundance of bows on one side, two on the back.

By the afternoon, four customers had drifted in, and Gabe cooked hamburgers and fed them. Ben disappeared out to the shed and Seagull. Katie and Will went back upstairs. Annie heard their giggles, and then they were quiet.

If it hadn't been Christmas, she would have been upstairs in a flash. Silence was unnerving for a parent. She'd seen Katie's conspiratorial peek around the door, heard Will's request of Gabe for a pencil.

They were making Christmas.

At four, Ben stamped back in the back door, scraping his boot heels against the stoop as he shucked off his coat and slicked back his hair. ''Weather's changing. Might get a frost tonight.''

The fabric of his black shirt strained against his shoulders. Annie remembered how his muscles had coiled against her hands, coiled and bunched as he'd held her. She looked away from him, from the power implicit in his every move and down at the stack of hot dogs she was stringing together to make a facsimile crown roast for Christmas dinner.

''The orange groves will be in trouble if the temperature drops another few degrees.''

''Don't think so.'' Gabe had his foot propped on the rung of a chair. ''Radio said no frost warnings are out.''

"Oh?" Ben came into the bar, and Annie smelled the clean, cool air clinging to his shirt, the scent of pine. "Good. I thought I might have to keep a watch out during the night for our own trees."

A hot dog slid sideways as Annie ran a string through it half an inch from the bottom end.

"What's that?" Ben pointed to the upright circle of hot dogs. Unlike his dress shirts, the black work shirt fit snugly over his belly, outlining his flat stomach.

"Dinner," Annie muttered.

"What's wrong with steak?" He took two steps closer to her and stopped, as if he, too, had drawn a line he didn't want to cross on this day. "I'm not complaining, mind you."

"Good. Don't," Annie said, unable to avoid noticing the way his faded jeans slid over his thighs. The thread slipped out of her fingers and the circle of hot dogs fanned flat. "Darn it."

"Them four that showed up ate the last steaks and ordered burgers to go. We're plumb out of beef. I meant to go over to Duke's ranch yesterday and pick up more. I forgot." Gabe looked sheepishly at her. "We get all our beef from Duke. That's why our burgers are so good."

Annie went back to work.

Strung together with string half an inch at top and bottom, the hot dogs were a circle of meat with an empty center. She needed stuffing. Apples. Sauerkraut. Something for the center. Contemplating the hot dogs, she frowned and tilted her head to one side, trying to think of something that would fill that empty hole.

Reaching over her shoulder, Ben nudged one of the hot dogs. The circle stayed firm. "We have a lot of hamburger buns in the storeroom."

"Onions?"

"In the freezer. Breaded."

"You can scrape the breading off." She slipped past him, allowing herself only a small inhalation of his clean scent. It was Christmas, after all, and she deserved a present, too.

He dropped his hand. "I'm going up to change." He vanished.

The pile of presents under the tree had increased by the time Josh wafted through the door, cold air circling around him. Mike was next, elegant in a dark blue suit. Josh and Mike added to the modest collection under the tree.

"Merry Christmas, y'all," Josh whooped.

Her eyes wide and distressed, Katie dragged Will upstairs again.

Annie chopped up onion rings and mushrooms, stirring them into the butter she'd melted in a pan. Running back from the pantry with a bag of buns in her hand, she bounced off Ben's solid chest.

Grabbing her elbows, he kept her upright. "Slow down, Annie. It's no big deal."

"That's what I said," she retorted and blushed violently as she remembered the context of her remark. Tearing herself free of his grip, she slid to a stop at the burner with her mushrooms and onions and grabbed the pan handle. "Oh! Dirty word, dirty word," she said, shaking her hand.

As she turned, Ben wrapped her hand in a dishrag filled with ice. "Easy to get burned, Annie."

And she knew he wasn't talking about a frying pan filled with onions and mushrooms.

"I'll finish," Josh boomed, using up the last of the free space in the narrow aisle.

Crammed against the bar, Annie was nose to nose once more with Ben, every inch of him pressed against her as he held her hand ceilingward.

"Oh, Annie, we've got to stop meeting like this," he murmured.

Annie had never imagined how appealing Ben Jackson could be when there was mischief in his hazel eyes. Sur-

ounded by his masculine scent, feeling the strength of his
highs against hers, she couldn't breathe.

"In shock, Angel-Annie?" he murmured in the vicinity
of her buzzing ears as Josh bumped Ben closer.

Maybe she was.

"You need to lower your head."

The teasing note drifted away, an illusion, she thought
dizzily as he stepped back, still holding her arm upright
while Josh stirred the pan of vegetables behind them.

"I think I need to sit down," Annie said, and did, dropping her head between her knees as she collapsed onto the
chair solicitously extended by Mike.

With her head down, Annie saw Ben's highly polished
shoes exit through the door to the storeroom.

After running cold water over her blistered palm, Annie
let the elderly trio crumble bread into her mix of onions and
mushrooms while she supervised.

Katie and Will came in from outside with some kind of
holly berries they'd discovered in the backyard.

Placing one spray on each table, they saved two large
sprigs for the doors. "Mistletoe," said Katie as Josh held
her up to the top of the storeroom door frame. Her red ribbon hung limply from her unraveling braid.

After Annie slid the crown roast of hot dogs one-handed
into the oven to cook for twenty minutes, she excused herself and went upstairs.

The fluttery excitement she'd felt from the moment she'd
come downstairs had lingered. That sense of her world
trembling on the brink of something momentous had stayed
with her all day. She'd always associated that trembling
sense of anticipation with the holidays.

In spite of everything, Christmas was happening.

Rummaging through her suitcase, she found what she was
looking for. The day deserved her best green dress. And gold
star earrings.

Dressing rapidly, Annie stopped at one point and flattened her open hand against her stomach to still the quivers as she heard the laughter from downstairs.

Gabe and his friends, Will, Katie and she sat down to the crown roast with its stuffing, a bowl of baked beans, and sliced tomatoes wheeled over the last of the lettuce.

Josh had poured beer into mugs and made ginger ale with maraschino cherries for Katie and Will.

The three men didn't mention Ben's absence.

Waiting for Gabe to say he'd go find Ben, Annie wanted to tell them to stop, tell them that it wasn't right to leave Ben out. She stood, ready to go looking for him, not about to accept that he would remain aloof from their make-do celebration.

She wanted him with them. The day would be ruined without him, all that lovely anticipation going flat like the opened ginger ale, the bubbles disappearing.

"Don't, Annie." Gabe shook his head. "Ben will be all right. He doesn't like fusses. And we've done nothing but fuss all day. He went out to the shed."

"Don't you dare lift one fork until I bring him back," Annie ordered, racing outside.

She saw the gleam of his shirt in the near darkness of the shed.

Dressed in his formal shirt, dark slacks and polished shoes, Ben sat in the cold on a wooden box inside the shed. He stroked the nose of the old horse and let it nibble on a carrot he held out.

"What do you think you're doing, Ben Jackson?" Annie was furious.

"Pretty obvious, isn't it, angel?" He held up the carrot. "Feeding Seagull."

"Listen to me." Keeping her knees off the dirt of the shed floor, Annie knelt beside him. "You can't do this."

"Well, actually, I can." His expression was somber.

"I won't let you ruin Christmas for everyone in there."

"Angel, I'm not ruining anything for anybody. I want to be out here."

Annie bit her lip at the loneliness in his voice. She didn't know what had put it there, and she didn't think she could bear the bleakness in his hard face. She knew, *knew* with a bone-deep conviction that the best place for Ben Jackson this Christmas was inside with Gabe and his wise guys, with her children, with *her,* not outside with Seagull.

"I know it's not a fancy meal, and except for me and the kids, none of us are family, and the children and I have intruded into your life and turned it upside down." She patted his cheek, much as Katie had tapped hers earlier in the day. "But it's *Christmas,* Ben." She wanted to take his lonely, shuttered face and draw it to her, offer a comfort she knew he'd reject.

Instead, she brushed his smooth, short hair back, watching it fall into place as she said, "Please don't stay out here in the cold, Ben. We want you with us. Gabe does. The children do."

He captured her hand and lifted it, turning it palm up against his mouth. "And what about you, Annie? Do you want me at the groaning board, too?"

"Yes," she murmured, spellbound as he closed her fist around the kiss he'd pressed there. "It won't be Christmas without you, Ben."

"That's funny, Annie," he said, but there was no mirth in his low voice.

"Why? I don't understand." She rushed into speech, frantic to persuade him that he would be missed. "No matter what you insist, Gabe and Mike and Josh are your friends. You own the Star—"

"Shh." He touched one long finger to her lips and ran his hand over her hair, stroking it as he'd earlier stroked Seagull's nose. "You would never understand, Annie."

"Of course I would." She curved her cheek to his stroking hand, aching for him.

"No, Gabe had it right the first time. You're like the angel that walked in through the front door of the Star, light and hope, and all that radiance glowing from you." He lifted her hair at the nape of her neck and spread it between his fingers before he withdrew his hand. "Did you know that even in this shed, Annie, you glow? Your pretty green dress shimmers and shines, and there's nothing else here except you and your gold star earrings glowing and sparkling like the last light in a dying town."

Annie wanted to weep for the desolation she heard in his harsh voice. Gathering her courage, though, she taunted him, knowing she was risking that whole tremulous feeling she'd carried around inside her all day. "You'd prefer to be the ghost at our feast, then? Have every bite of our delicious meal—and you'll be missing a treat if you don't have your share of that crown roast—turn to ashes in our mouths? And don't you *dare* say we won't miss you, and we'll enjoy our dinner without you. Because we won't." She felt like stamping her foot and adding "so there," but she didn't.

"All right, I won't say that, Annie." He stood up, regretfully, and brushed off the seat of his slacks. "I don't want to be the ghost at anybody's banquet table. I won't do that to you. Come on. We'll have your Christmas dinner and unwrap the presents."

Striding ahead of her, a broad dark presence in the twilight, he lacked only the cape and scythe to complete the image of the Grim Reaper, she thought, as she followed him into the Star.

They had waited for her to return. The stunned expressions on the faces of Gabe and his cronies told her they hadn't, however, expected her to return with Ben, who sat down next to her, his black and white a somber note among the bright reds and greens she and the children wore. The splashy Hawaiian print shirts Gabe and Josh had donned seemed holiday-cheerful in spite of their tropical casualness. And Mike had lightened the formality of his suit with a red-and-green-striped tie and a rose pinned to his lapel.

They spooned out the stuffing from the center of the crown roast of wieners, opened Ben a beer and toasted the holiday. Ben drank with them, and if he didn't repeat the "here, here" the rest of them said, Annie believed she was the only one who noticed.

He tried, he really tried not to be the ghost at the feast and his effort came close to breaking her heart. The more they laughed and joked, the quieter he became. They roared with laughter when the hot dogs fell apart after Annie cut the strings running through their ends. Ben smiled, oh, she could see that, but his eyes withdrew to some other place, their hazel gleam dulling as the evening lengthened.

Annie brought out the pink ladies and brandy alexanders she'd concocted earlier after searching high and low for ice cream. With the Christmas-pink of the grenadined pink ladies and the green of the brandy alexanders she'd tinted with crème de menthe, the dessert drinks brought "ohs" and "whoopees" as she brought them out on a foil-covered tray.

For Katie and Will, Annie had dipped the ice cream into wineglasses and topped their servings with strawberry jelly she'd found in the back of the Star's refrigerator, and they "ooh-ed" and "ah-ed" when she put their dishes in front of them.

Handing Ben a long-handled spoon for his dessert, she wished she could see his eyes. Remote, he was there, but he clenched the spoon a little too tightly, said "thank-you" a bit too politely.

When Josh lumbered over to the lopsided tree and scooped up the presents, Katie leaned over to Annie and, close to her ear, whispered, "Mr. Josh is really Santa Claus, Mommy. Only in disguise. Like in the movie last night."

"I don't think so," Annie whispered back, watching the tips of Josh's ears turn red as he overheard Katie's whisper.

As Josh handed around the assortment of strangely wrapped presents, Ben stretched his legs to one side of the table, tipping back toward the storeroom and away from the table with its dishes and centerpiece of gherkin trees and berry sprigs.

Folding his arms across his chest, he seemed to disappear into the darkness at the corner of the room.

Annie's heart went out to him.

Watching him as she spooned her brandy alexander into her mouth, Annie felt that quivery fluttering inside her swelling and blooming.

Will unwrapped his large, lumpy, newspaper-covered present first. The wrinkles around Gabe's eyes swallowed up his laughing eyes as Will pulled back the paper.

Speechless, Will sat and stared at the object on the table. The alligator's jaws were closed, the eye sockets vacant. Up close, the skull was even more impressive than it had been hanging on the wall next to the clock under the stained-glass window. Poking his finger through the socket, Will murmured reverently, "*Wowohwow*. Oh, boy."

She'd found a pack of baseball cards she'd tucked away in one of the boxes from their apartment and she'd wrapped the pack in a five dollar bill, but baseball cards weren't in the same neighborhood as the bleached-out, cleaned-up bones of a very large, very ugly alligator skull.

She knew Will would drag it into bed with them if she let him. She knew, too, the skull had been Gabe's idea.

For Katie, she'd torn apart one of her own blouses and sewed Armadillo two dresses, a ball gown edged with the lace from one of Annie's slips and a school dress for the doll to wear when Katie started her new school after the holidays.

Josh and Mike had found a convenience store open, they declared as the children unwrapped wooden paddles and

ed-and-white-striped plastic candy canes filled with round
hocolate candies and peppermints.

Katie and Will had made silver stars out of aluminum foil
or Mike and Josh, and the two men smiled and sent Gabe
or sticky tape so that they could wear their stars on their
hirts for the rest of the evening.

There were three presents left, and Josh handed Katie the
ne that had been lying on the bar since morning. Slowly
ulling the newspaper back, Katie looked down at the hula
oll, and when she looked up, her gaze flew straight to Ben.
Iolding the garish doll carefully in her arms, Katie walked
ver to Ben and climbed on his lap. "This is the best Kiss-
nus ever." She kissed him on the cheek and rested her head
gainst him as she touched the doll's curls and skirt.

Annie thought she saw Ben's arms jerk, almost as if he
vanted to close them around Katie, but he didn't, merely sat
here silently while she admired her doll. When Katie
limbed down and went to look under the Christmas tree on
he bar, Ben edged his chair farther away from the table.

But Will and Katie had their own gifts to give.

First Will, then Katie, handed Gabe a poem. Her chil-
ren trotted next to Ben, handing him his poem. The po-
ms were wrapped carefully, if clumsily, in aluminum foil
tched with stars and snowflakes. Gabe read his aloud and
ave the children hugs.

Ben read his silently. Afterward, he folded the foil slowly
ack over the red-crayoned paper and looked at Annie.

His smile, beautiful and sad, made her heart turn over.

Katie and Will handed Annie two identical packages. The
oil-covered small boxes were tied with the remains of one
f Katie's green hair ribbons, the uneven edges shredded by
he repeated attempts to get the bow "just so," as Will said.

When she started to untie the bow of one box, Will made
er read the folded piece of paper that came with it first. *Do
ot unwrap. This box holds all my love which is inside. Your
on, Will.* Annie was informed that the squiggles on Katie's

note carried the same message. "Only not 'your son, Will,'"
Katie said. "*Mine* says, *Your Katie*. Right there." She
pointed to a wavering long line.

Annie swallowed and pulled them to her. "You've made
this the best Christmas I've ever had. Thank you, sweet-
hearts." Looking up through damp eyelashes, Annie saw
Ben watching her from the gloom of the doorway between
the room and the staircase. "I love you more than anything
in the whole world," she breathed through the joy swelling
through her.

Josh and Mike left for home shortly afterward, and Gabe
disappeared upstairs to bed.

Annie led her unwilling children to their bed, Will cart-
ing the alligator skull as she'd known he would, Katie
clutching her "princess." When she returned downstairs to
clean up, Ben was still there, loading the dishwasher, des-
ultorily picking up bits and pieces of torn newspaper.

"I didn't expect you to come back downstairs," he said,
the wet wineglass he held dripping onto the floor.

"I thought I'd do the cleaning up," she said, and their
words overlapped.

"Well—" He switched a wineglass awkwardly from one
hand to the other. "You cooked. I'll clean." He closed his
broad hands around her waist and lifted her up onto the bar.

"I don't know about this arrangement," she said, uncomfortable with the idea of sitting idly by while he did the
dishes and put away the remains of the food.

"You'll be fine." Bending over, he spoke to her somewhere from under the bar, the wide triangle of his shoulders tapering to the narrow black belt around his waist. He
straightened and walked over to her.

Annie plucked nervously at the ends of the Christmas tree
at her side.

But he lifted the tray of dishes and carted them to the
sink, scraping off food and rinsing them before stacking
them in the dishwasher, his movements smooth and prac-

iced. He didn't move with her roller-coaster rapidity, but with his measured, controlled, deceptively slow motions he accomplished as much as she did.

Annie inhaled the smells of peppermint and chocolate from the candy canes the kids had opened. In the dim light of the bar, she realized she was happy, and she flung her arms wide. "I love Christmas," she murmured.

"I don't. It's only another day." Pausing in front of her with the bean dish in one hand, Ben lifted his other and brushed her cheek with the back of his hand. "You're something special, Annie Conroy. You came in here and you made a holiday out of nothing. You really care about all this phony Christmas stuff, don't you?"

Swinging her feet, Annie considered her answer. She wanted him to understand how it was for her, and so she spoke reflectively. "It's more than religion for me, Ben. I love this time of year, the lights, the sense of anticipation. The excitement of all the colors. And, yes, I love giving presents and trying to make the day into a special celebration."

"Well," he observed, shrugging, "you made today special for Gabe and the old guys. And for your children."

"But not for you, did I, Ben?" Annie asked gently. "This was an ordeal for you, wasn't it?"

"Yeah." Balling his fists into her skirt on either side of her, he pinned her to the bar. "Rituals aren't my thing."

"It's more than hating rituals, though, isn't it?" Dragged downward by his fists doubled into its skirt, her dress became too tight in the front. The small gold buttons running from neckline to hem strained at the bodice, in danger of sliding free of the buttonholes, and she shifted, trying to ease the fabric. "You don't have to be religious to feel the wonder of the season, the way the earth moves from the shortest day and the longest night toward light. Toward the sun. That's reason enough to celebrate, Ben, the idea that winter is coming to an end. Why do you hate Christmas?"

He was silent for so long that she didn't know if he'd heard her.

"All right, angel." His words were dangerously soft, and she felt the anger and bitterness rising toward her in one enormous wave. "I'll tell you about Christmas Past. But Dickens gave his characters a happy ending. This is a story with no ending, only a beginning."

Swallowing Annie said, "I'm listening." She placed her hand flat against his thundering heart. She wasn't going to like this story. She knew that. But he'd warned her.

And she wanted to know. She needed to know what kept him locked away in some lonely place where he allowed no one in, a place where darkness trapped him.

"Tell me the story, Ben." Giving him a gift he neither recognized nor wanted, Annie wrapped her arms around his shoulders, holding him in the shadows of the Star.

Chapter Ten

So, holding Angel-Annie captive between his arms, Ben told her.

"A long time ago," he began, doubling his fists tighter as all the old anger and grief roared through him, "there was a young boy."

"Go on, Ben." Annie leaned toward him, her small breasts tender and soft against him and he wanted to warn her away, but he'd tried, over and over, he'd warned her, with his actions, with his words.

"Annie, you don't want to hear this story." He touched her forehead, cool and smooth, with his hot cheek. "You want everything bright and cheerful. And you work so hard, against all kinds of odds to give your children happy ever after. Believe me, you don't want to hear this."

"Believe me, I do." Her breath was fragrant with peppermint.

Ben felt as if all the ugliness inside him would come spilling out over her, Annie in her Christmas dress with its sleeves curving over the points of her shoulders. He kissed the slope of one shoulder where the small sleeve had drooped down and looked past her to the flickering neon star outside the room. The lights glowing on the jukebox were muted and an old song wove around them.

If he knew how to let it in, all that radiance he felt in her would shine away the darkness holding him in its depths.

Straightening her sleeve so that it covered her again, Ben continued, dealing out his words one by one. "My mother was a professional dancer, Annie. She loved to dance. She loved music, and she loved to laugh. She was the happiest person I've ever met."

Lifting Annie into his arms, wrapping her legs around him, Ben walked out from behind the bar. "Dance with me, Annie, while I tell you the rest of the story. Let me hold you, like this." She murmured something, and he pulled her closer, holding her to him as he moved to the slow, slow strains of the song.

Shutting his eyes, he remembered and told her about the boy. "My father. Well, angel, my father didn't like much of anything. Except being left alone. Left alone to drink. Night after night, angel, all alone at the kitchen table, he'd drink."

The music ended as Ben circled near the jukebox. Opening his eyes, he pushed another button, setting it to repeat the songs. Letting the music fill the room, he danced with Annie in and out of the neon colors patterning the floor.

"And one day, my mother quit laughing so much. Oh, she still smiled. I gave her the hula doll. She smiled then. But she didn't dance anymore. Except with me. During all those long nights, she'd put on a tape, and we'd dance."

"You're a good dancer." Annie's breath tickled his ear. Her hair was soft against his cheek, tangling in his mouth as she moved her face.

"While my father drank, angel, we'd dance. She taught me all the old dances." Ben let Annie slide to the floor, her slight body trembling all the way down his, and he took one of her hands in his, held her waist, such a small waist it was, too, and dipped with her, raised her and twirled her to the slow strains of the song.

"And then one night, he took a bat and smashed the tape recorder. We didn't dance anymore after that." Ben placed his cheek against Annie's and danced her sideways, tango-position, down the middle of the room.

"Oh, Ben—"

"There's not much more, angel." He held her arm vertically and spun her once, twice, and back to him. "Then the Christmas I was eight—"

"Ah," she said, and tears polished her pale cheeks. "I know how this story ends."

"No," he chided, dipping her again, watching the lights in her hair. "I told you. This is a story that doesn't have an ending."

"Tell me the middle, then."

"That Christmas, my mother had wrapped all the presents and put them under the tree. We were going to open them early, before the old man started drinking. He was okay, not so bad when he was sober. During the days he usually was. It was the nights. That was when he drank, Annie."

"I'm sorry, Ben, sorry for all of that, sorry I made you tell me this if you don't want to." She rubbed her eyes against his shirt.

"I think I wanted to tell you. I've never told anyone *all* of the story though Gabe knows most of it." Ben closed his eyes again and turned and turned, holding her, breathing in her pepperminty scent, her sweet Annie-scent. "We came into breakfast. The old man was slouched at the table, a cup of coffee between his hands. He looked at my mother, at the tree, at me. Then he got up, took the cup to the sink, rinsed it and walked out. I never saw him again. He didn't say one word. He just shook his head and walked out."

The beat of the new song was faster, and Ben held Annie in one place, swaying to the rhythm.

"At first I was happy. But my mother sat at the kitchen table all day, staring at that damned silver tree with the lights flashing on it and the presents underneath. Finally, she got up and packed all the presents away. She said we'd wait for a while to celebrate Christmas. We'd wait until the old man came home. Well, angel, he didn't come home, and we never celebrated Christmas again. Instead, every holiday my mother and I would go early in the day to whatever bar was open. She'd sit there, me at her side, and watch the people who came in and out. We'd stay there all day. I'd play games, cards with whoever showed up, anything to make the day pass faster."

"That's why you keep the Star open? Because of your mother?" Annie's voice was a silk thread wrapping around him, binding him to her.

"I don't know. I always thought she expected the old man to show up in one of those bars one Christmas."

"You were only eight." Annie kneaded his shoulders. "A year older than Will. You're breaking my heart, Ben."

"Yeah? Well, that's the last thing I want to do." He swung her wide and around the room, back to the wooden bar where he ended as he'd begun, standing in front of her, his fists curled in the silky fabric of her green dress. "And when I was fourteen, she faded away. The last time I saw her smile was when I gave her the doll. She went six years without laughing or smiling, and then she died, all the joy and hope long-gone."

He unbuttoned and rebuttoned the tiny gold ball at the neckline of Annie's dress.

"What happened to you?" She framed his face with her cool, trembling hands.

"Oh, I shuffled between whatever set of relatives felt like putting up with a surly teenage boy. Babies are like kittens. Everybody loves them. Teenage boys are like full-grown cats, Annie. Not everybody has a soft spot for a rebellious adolescent hell-bent on self-destruction. And there usually wasn't enough money for clothes. You know how teenagers are. I was tough enough that most of the kids left me alone, but I'd hear them laughing when the soles of my shoes came loose and flapped against the stairs when I walked up them.''

"You're right. I don't understand how anybody could let you go to school like that. I would give up everything I owned if Will or Katie needed shoes." She drummed her fists against his arm. "I wish I'd been around," she said fiercely. "I wouldn't have let people treat you like that."

"After a couple of years, I lied about my age and joined the army. And that's that, angel. A story with no ending. Well, one ending. I took a graduation equivalency degree so I'd be able to say I completed high school, and since I passed the college entrance tests, I went to college with my army money. I don't know if my old man's alive or dead, I don't know why he walked out on us, and you know something, Angel-Annie? I don't give a damn."

The last song ended before he did, and Ben was startled to hear his last words loud in the silence.

"My father destroyed everything bright and good in my mother, Annie, and everybody always said I was the spitting image of my old man. I hated him with every cell in my body while I was growing up. They said I'm just like him. So I stay away from shining, fragile things, angel." Ben tugged her to him and kissed her, kissed her for all the Christmases he'd never had, kissed her for all the ones he wouldn't have.

Her cheek was damp and cool and he tasted her tears on the tip of his tongue as she kissed him back. But he'd said he didn't want her gratitude and meant it. And he didn't want her pity, either. So, smoothing her shiny hair back from her tear-wet face, he lifted her down from his well-polished bar. "Go to bed, Annie. Christmas is over."

Waking up the next morning, Annie avoided Ben, knowing intuitively that he wouldn't want to be reminded that he'd told her his story with no ending. It haunted her, and she couldn't forget it.

The snap and crackle between them was so powerful that she knew she needed time to put what he'd told her about himself into perspective.

What he'd revealed explained his shuttered loneliness, his highly polished shoes and austere, formal style of clothes.

During the week between Christmas and New Year's, she watched him and wept for the lost child he'd been, watched him with her own children, his awkwardness with them, until her heart finally cracked in two.

But she understood even more clearly that she couldn't help him. Despite his insistence that he didn't care what had happened to his father, Annie knew Ben was lying to himself. He cared so much about the unsolved mystery of his past that he couldn't live in the present. No one could help him. He had to reach out himself and escape the past, had to go beyond his sense of inevitable self-destruction. No one could wave a magic wand over him and make all the pain go away.

The more she watched Ben, the more she understood the thickness of the masks he wore. His brusque treatment of Gabe masked the way he watched over the old man. His quiet reserve with the customers only drew them to him. Women left their phone numbers on the bar under their napkins and he waited until they'd left before sweeping the scribbled numbers into the trash. And people *talked* to him. They confided in him the most unbelievably private aspects of their lives. She understood that, too. The promise of strength in his craggy face and in his solid body invited people to lean on him.

But he didn't lean back. He kept his distance.

And after Christmas night, Annie found that he avoided her, too. Before Christmas when they'd tried so hard to stay out of each other's reach, they'd kept colliding.

Now, she saw him only during the hours when the Star was open. The space behind the bar seemed to have become as large as a football field, even on the days Josh pitched in and cooked.

She told herself she was glad.

But she found herself listening for the creak of the boards in the hall under his feet when he passed her bedroom at night. She told herself it was compassion, fellow-feeling.

Annie knew she was lying to herself when she realized she missed bumping into Ben Jackson, craved his callused hands under her elbows, steadying her. She missed the magnetic turning of her body to his, the humming along her nerve ends every time he came near her.

She missed *him*.

He'd heard the unvoiced fears of her son and given Will a chance to remember for a short while that he was, after all, a child. Reserved, wary, Ben Jackson had been a mirror to Katie, reflecting to her small daughter a sense of what she *could* be.

He'd carefully salvaged her Christmas bows from the dirt, dropping them one by one like presents into her lap, and she'd fallen in love with him.

The mustard bottle slipped through her suddenly nerveless fingers onto the bar and clattered to the edge.

As she'd watched him, seeing beyond the guarded wall to his kindness and his loneliness, she'd recognized the need in him and somehow, in spite of all the reasons not to, she'd grown to love him.

With an unsteady hand, Annie caught the mustard. She had to leave as soon as Gabe could finish the repair on her car. If she didn't . . .

Going out to the backyard where Gabe had parked the car, Annie saw Will and Gabe engrossed in conversation underneath the hood. Their heads were plunged deep inside the bowels of her car's engine and their remarkably similar skinny behinds waggled over the front.

"I know Skeeter told you that. He was right, too. But let me show you another way to kill a goose, young Will. Sometimes old age teaches a body a trick or two you young folks haven't learned. A trick I'll bet even Skeeter doesn't know. *Ouch!* Hand me that socket wrench, Will."

Will pulled his head out from under the car hood. "Hi, Mom."

"Hi." She patted his shoulder and let him dive back under the hood.

During the last week, *mommy* had become *mom*.

Seeing the anxiety fade day by day from Will's tightly strung body, Annie wasn't able to regret the change. Gabe—and Ben—had been good for her son.

He'd insisted on weeding around the Star, but Ben had paid Will, not letting the boy turn his work into an "even trade." Will stacked his coins up and then exchanged them with Ben at the bar for dollar bills. He had five dollars, and every night he laid out his money, counting it, recounting it, making plans.

Unfortunately, his plans all centered on the Star and Seagull. Will hadn't made any plans for using his money after they left.

Sometimes Annie didn't feel like making any more plans, either, but she'd known from the first that the situation was temporary, hadn't wanted it to be anything *but* temporary until Ben Jackson had taken over her brain, wandering in and out at will.

With her sneaker-clad toe, she dug up a clot of grass. Darn the man, anyway. Tamping the grass back in place, she caught Gabe looking at her, his eyes shrewd.

"Bet you got something you want to talk with me about, huh?"

Annie shrugged. "How's the car coming?"

"Once the control module comes in, we'll have 'er fixed up quick as a wink."

Remembering some of Gabe's sly and very slow winks, Annie didn't feel reassured. "Will, run back and check on Katie, please, while I talk to Gabe."

"Hecky-durn." Will stomped away, a greasy rag trailing from his back pocket.

"Sorry, Miss Annie, but I told him he couldn't say 'hell's bells' even if I did, so the cherub come up with that phrase."

"Don't worry about it," she said, and Gabe's cackling echo followed on her last syllable.

They laughed.

"So, what's on your mind, Miss Annie, besides that horse's hind end I call my partner?" Gabe wiped his face with the mate to Will's greasy rag.

"It's time for me and the children to go, Gabe."

"Figured that was why you come out here with such a long face. The old Star kinda grows on you, don't it?"

"I have to find a place to live, a *job*, and the children need to be back in school after New Year's. I thought—" she scuffed the ground, raising dust clouds "—maybe we should get an early start? Get settled?"

The tap of the socket wrench against Gabe's leg filled the silence between them.

"If that's what you want." His skinny body slumped. "I like your kids, Miss Annie, and I like you. You know you're welcome to stay. Kids could go to school here."

"I know." Annie stuffed her hands into her pockets. "But we can't."

"Give me until the day after New Year's. I can have your car ready by then."

"Let me know as soon as you can how much I owe you."

"Sure. Whatever you say." Gabe stuck his head back under the hood.

Staying downstairs after cleanup, she told Ben that night she and the children would leave after New Year's.

"Yeah?" He nodded and twisted the tie around the neck of the garbage sack. "Did you tell Gabe?"

Nodding, Annie handed Ben the bin of cans.

"What did he say?"

"Oh, you know Gabe." Annie didn't want to tell Ben that Gabe wanted them to stay longer. "He said he'd have the car ready."

"Annie—"

"What?" She paused, not knowing what she hoped he would say, but she wanted the awkwardness ended between them.

"Nothing." He tossed the sack of garbage on top of the bin and carried them toward the storeroom. "Whatever you want is all right with me."

She had more trouble with Katie and Will. They didn't understand. Katie became very quiet and stayed close by Ben's side. Will's anxiety lines reappeared, and Annie felt like the evil witch in the fairy tale. Except she didn't want to leave, either. And, like Katie, she wanted to trail beside Ben, following him around until...

And the rest of her thoughts made her more determined than ever to leave.

Late on New Year's Day, Mike and Josh came to the Star. Gabe had told them the Conroys were leaving and the men had come to say goodbye. Gabe and Ben watched as the wise guys said their farewells.

Mike handed her a long white envelope. "Mrs. Conroy, the three of us have a token of our appreciation for Christmas and New Year's dinner, and, too, we would like for you and the children to have something to tide you over until you find a job. Call it, perhaps, a holiday bonus."

"Ms. Annie, we pooled our resources and compiled a list of people we know in Azalea and in Palma de Flora who might have job openings. Palma de Flora is the better bet, though, I believe we're all in agreement?" Josh checked with Gabe and Mike. "We expect you to let us know if you have any problems. Will you?"

Muffled against his burly chest, Annie nodded. Maybe Katie was right and Josh was Santa Claus. "I will. I promise."

Slouched at the bar next to Ben, Gabe kept quiet while Mike shook her hand and Josh bear-hugged her again before leaving.

Twisting the strand of fake pearls that she'd knotted between her breasts, Annie tried not to think of how much she would miss Gabe and his friends.

And she was determined not to think about Ben Jackson.

"If we're going to get an early start, I'd better go on up."

"I'll fix breakfast in the morning," Gabe said, scowling.

"No, don't, please." Annie held out her hand. "Really. I'd rather stop somewhere and take a break after we've been driving for a while. It will be easier," she said gently as Gabe's face fell.

"Huh." Gabe turned and shuffled to the stairs. "I'll still be up. Old folks wake up early, you know, so it wouldn't be any trouble at all . . ." His words trailed up the stairs.

"You're dead-set on leaving, then?" Ben's shadow fell across her.

"Have to." Annie couldn't talk.

"Damn you, Annie. I wish you'd never walked into my bar." Ben's voice was harsh, raw with control. Arms crossed tightly, he paced from one end of the bar to the other until he finally stopped in front of her, facing her.

"Fate." Her knees buckling, Annie sank into the nearest chair.

Kneeling on the dusty floor in front of her, Ben took her hands into his. "Annie, if I were a different kind of man, if you were a different type of woman—"

"We're who we are," she said and curled her fingers around his. She'd craved his touch for days, and it was going to be harder than she'd imagined to be adult. Harder than she could have dreamed to walk away from Ben Jackson and his loneliness and never again experience the way his slightest touch ran through her like electricity.

She was doing what she had to, for Katie and Will, for herself. And for Ben.

But she hadn't known there would be so much pain.

"Annie, I'm a rock and roll kind of man, here today, gone tomorrow. Rootless. You're waltzes in the moonlight and hundred-year-old trees. I like to pick up and go whenever and wherever the spirit moves me. I've never wanted to stay in one place too long. I don't like being tied down."

"Nobody's trying to tie you down, Ben," Annie said gently, hearing the pain behind his words, feeling the hunger in his tight grip of her hands. "You're as free as you've ever been, as free as you want to be."

"Hell, Annie. I'm not what you need." His words tumbled out, and she wanted to tell him how wrong he was. "All that glowing optimism, angel, I'd turn it inside out, just like my old man."

"You're wrong. But I can't rescue you, Ben. I tried that once, in my first marriage. If I could make you see what kind of man you really are, if I could make you see all the goodness and love inside you the way you made Katie see herself, I would. If I could show you the *real* man inside you, oh, Ben, I'd be your mirror for eternity." Annie clung to his forearms, and they trembled at her touch. "But *you* have to reach out. It has to be mutual, or it doesn't work."

"Angel." His chuckle was strained and raspy. "Some things would work, believe me."

"But not for long," she whispered, knowing she was right.

He stood up, dropping her hands. "No." He held his empty hands palms up. "You're the best thing that's ever happened to me, Annie Conroy, and I'm going to let you walk out my door. Crazy, right?" Ben shook his head. "Gabe is right. I'm a horse's hind end."

He touched her hair, his touch as light as the flutter of a moth's wing, and Annie ached with her yearning to throw good sense to the winds.

"If you stayed, Annie," he said softly, reading her mind, "the price would be too high. For me. For you." His hands slid along her arms. "*If*. What a powerful word, huh, angel?"

She'd thought he would kiss her, and she didn't think she could bear it.

He didn't. Not even the next morning when she started the engine. Standing at the front of the Star, the neon lights off, Ben and Gabe waited while the engine idled. Will and Katie were crying quietly and Annie wanted to sob, too, as she looked at Gabe's stooped old figure, wanted to climb out of the car and stay when she looked at Ben's shuttered expression.

She drove away, not looking once in her rearview mirror. She thought for a while that her windshield needed cleaning, but when she stopped to wipe it down, she felt her tears dropping against her hand and got back into the car.

Taking a deep breath, Annie left the Star behind her.

Ahead of her in the dawning sun, the road stretched long and empty.

Before Annie drove away, Ben turned on his heel and went back into the bar. He couldn't watch the three of them disappear into the sunrise. That much was beyond him.

Later in the day, as he walked past the bedroom where they'd stayed, he stepped into the room, drawn by a small box on the stripped bed.

The box was wrapped around and around with one of Annie's carefully tied red bows, one of the ones he'd helped her salvage. Ben picked up the box. Like the ones Katie and Will had given Annie, this one, too, was small and wrapped in foil. Stooping, he picked up the folded note that had drifted to the floor beside the bed.

Ben, the box is empty, of course. But anything is possible. I've always believed that. I still do.

Annie

Ben put the package on a shelf in his bedroom. Every morning the first things he saw were the glitter of the foil and the bright red, insistently cheerful ribbon.

The Star was packed every night with customers, but it seemed as empty as he felt inside. Like an automaton, he moved through the long nights, the flat days. The routine that had been so important failed him.

He dreamed. Not of the past, but of Annie. He woke up more tired than when he'd gone to bed. He missed her, missed her quicksilver movements, missed the glow that seemed to surround her.

After two weeks, the first letter came. Not to him. To Gabe, who shared it with Mike and Josh. The three of them scowled at Ben as he approached them, but he heard their muttered comments.

"... having trouble. What do you think?" They shut up when he stopped at the table.

"Letter from Annie?" Ben rolled the tray back and forth on the table.

"Yes, she wrote to us as we'd asked her," Mike said and offered nothing further.

If they didn't want to tell him how she was doing, Ben was damned if he'd ask.

By the end of January, though, he was fed up with half-heard comments. He'd heard Josh ask Gabe if Katie was still having the nightmares, but Ben hadn't heard Gabe's reply. One Sunday, Gabe's worried comment that Will was sick broke Ben's determination to keep his distance, and like a big old bass he snapped.

"All right. You win. What's going on with Annie and the kids?"

What they told him made him crazy with worry. Will was having some kind of serious medical crisis, Katie wouldn't go to school without screaming and Annie hadn't found a job. She was running out of money, but she'd found an apartment. "It has palmetto bugs that crawl out at night," Josh added. "We reckon that's why Katie's having nightmares."

Before Gabe disappeared upstairs later that night, Ben shoved a chair at him. "Sit down, old man. How bad is the situation for Annie?"

Shaking his head dolefully, Gabe said, "Dunno, not exactly. You know how the angel is. She don't say too much. We have to read between the lines."

"Can I see one of the letters?"

"Mike has the last one. He wanted to write her about some legal situation concerning her ex-husband." Gabe's rheumy blue eyes were filled with concern.

Having known the old man for four years, Ben figured he knew a con job when he heard one, but Gabe's comment about the legal situation disturbed him. "Look, Gabe, what can I do?"

"Hell's bells, old son. That's the easiest question anybody ever asked me. Go see for yourself how the angel and her cherubs are. You know you want to," he added slyly, not meeting Ben's eyes.

"Even if I did, what could I offer her? You know enough of my history. I'd walk out on her sooner or later. Like my old man."

"You think you're doomed to follow in that old rascal's footsteps, don't you, Benjamin Jackson?" For the first time since Ben had known Gabe, the old man was in a genuine, no-holds-barred rage. "You think you're a tumbling tumbleweed, too, huh?"

"You know what I am," Ben growled. "Nothing has—"

Gabe didn't give Ben time to complete his sentence. "Ever think why you polish that damned chunk of wood all the time?'' He pointed his bent finger to the long sweep of shining mahogany. Shuffling over to it, he thwacked it. "Real solid. Real stable. You brought the ugly old thing in here when it was scarred and gouged to a fare-thee-well. And Seagull. Don't forget the horse.''

"Yeah. So what's your point, old man?'' Ben tipped back on the legs of his chair.

Glowering at Ben, Gabe was silent, his chin quivering with fury. "There's that, too. You ever think why you call me 'old man' all the time? Think about it, *old son,* and while you're at it, why don't you go look up your *real* old man?''

Stomping off, his stooped shoulders hunched around his neck, Gabe left Ben speechless. Pausing at the arch between the storeroom and the bar area, Gabe shot his last cannonball. "And as far as what you got to offer that angel and her cherubs, shoot. You got yourself, your strong back, and a fair-to-middling education you earned yourself, even if you *don't* got a lick of good sense. And this old place don't have to stay a broken-down bar, unless that's how you want to keep it.''

It took Ben until the first week in February before he located his father's address, and he had to call in every favor he'd ever done anyone with access to public records, but he had the address typed out on a sheet of paper in his room.

Annie's red-ribboned foil box rested on top of the typed paper.

Ben left the paper on the shelf for four days.

Knowing the address was in Ben's possession, Gabe groused and complained, muttered and swore.

One night, fed up with the old man's constant nagging, Ben said, "Tomorrow. I'll go tomorrow and see him. Satisfied?''

"Yep.'' Gabe beamed.

"I don't want you to go with me." Ben scowled at Gabe who, having gotten his own way, was now prepared to let bygones be bygones.

"Don't want to go. That's between you and your old man."

When Ben drove into the trailer park outside Naples the next day, his hands were sweaty. He wanted to put his fist through the car windshield. He turned into the trailer park and drove past the address he'd been given, drove right back to the highway and headed home, to the Star.

But he couldn't forget Annie's note. And he wasn't sure the mischievous trio of old men were pulling a con on him.

And, finally, he knew Annie had been right. No one could rescue him. He had to dig his way up out of the darkness. No one could do it for him.

Knocking on the jalousied door of the trailer, Ben waited to see the huge bulk of his father. The frail, white-haired old man who answered the door was a stranger.

Checking the address again, Ben said, "Mr. Jackson?"

"Yes?"

This stranger, after all, was his father.

The harsh, withdrawn man who'd bulked larger than life for most of his thirty-two years, was, in reality, only this leathery, wizened stranger.

"I'm Ben."

"Ben?" No recognition showed in the man's face. "Do I know you?"

No, Ben almost said. "I'm your son. Ben. Ben Jackson."

"Come in." The old man held the door open, and Ben walked into the past.

The main living area of the trailer was neat. There were no personal mementos around. The room reminded him of his own bedroom.

"What do you want, Ben?" His father bent into a chair.

Ben hadn't planned what he was going to say, but the words were there, and he didn't have to search for them. Perhaps they'd been there for twenty-four years, been in the back of his mind since the old man had walked quietly out the front door and disappeared.

"I want you to tell me why you tossed me and my mother aside with less thought than you'd use to trade in a used car." Sitting on the couch, Ben waited. He'd waited twenty-four years for the answer, he could wait all day if necessary, now that he'd asked the question.

"That was a long time ago." The old man frowned. "I don't remember much about those days." He shrugged. "I remember you and your ma liked to dance all the time. She was a beautiful woman, your ma." The old man furrowed his brow, making an effort. "You were a quiet kid. I remember that. Not much more. I'm sorry." He stood up. His knees creaked. "Can I get you a glass of iced tea? No?" He sat back down. "That's all I can offer you. I don't encourage company dropping in. I like my solitude." Ben's father folded his hands over his knees. "Was there anything else you wanted to know?"

But Ben had found out everything he needed to know. He'd gone looking for his father and discovered a stranger who wanted nothing more than solitude. Well, he'd gotten it.

With the sunlight streaming through the trailer door, Ben suddenly knew with absolute certainty that he didn't want solitude. He wanted Annie and all her glowing warmth, he wanted Katie and her mischievous grin, he wanted to see Will lose the worry lines in his childish face. He wanted them, all of them, in his life.

Ben laughed.

The man who was his father was nothing like him, not in the least like Ben, who'd created a family out of a decrepit bar, turned a crabby, rheumy-eyed old man into a substi-

ute father, and made a pet out of a knock-kneed horse no
one else wanted.

Someday he might want to visit his *real* old man again.
But he didn't *need* to. It wouldn't matter one way or the
other.

He was free.

Driving home, Ben felt as if the weight of the world had
rolled off his shoulders and he'd stepped into the light. All
around him the sun was blazing down and he lifted his face
to it, loving it.

He made one stop before he turned the car in the direction of Palma de Flora.

When the doorbell rang, Annie fastened the slinky red
belt she'd looped through the waistband of her black, cuffed
shorts. She couldn't find her shoes, and the doorbell kept up
its nagging buzz. "Help!" She grabbed the ties at the end of
her red-and-white shirt, pulling the ends tightly into a bow
as she opened the door. Her dangling red-heart earrings
banged against her chin as she stepped back in shock.

"Ben Jackson. As I live and breathe," she said, echoing
his earlier teasing. Only she couldn't. Her breath was caught
somewhere deep inside and she wondered if she were going
to fall over in a heap at his polished loafers.

"Weren't expecting me, I reckon?"

"No," she rattled, her breath still hitching in her chest.
"Is Gabe all right?"

"He is now, but he won't be when I get back to the Star,"
Ben said with an assessing glance around the small living
room. Not waiting for an invitation, he strolled into her
kitchen and studied the drawings stuck to the refrigerator
door. "Nice." He fingered the edges of a yellow-and-purple
flower Katie had drawn at kindergarten. "How are Katie's
nightmares?"

"Excuse me?"

"Katie's nightmares," he said politely. "And the pa
metto bugs? Did you finally get rid of them?" he saic
coming toward her and toying with the tag ends of her bow

His knuckles brushed her tummy, and that old devi
quivering started again, the quivering that had kept he
sleepless for over a month whenever she thought about Be
Jackson, which, she thought indignantly as he continued t
walk her backward through her kitchen, had seemed to t
every hour of every day.

"Why are you here, Ben?" Annie was afraid to know
afraid to hope. She had too much at stake to be a fool fc
love.

"Thought maybe you needed some help taking Will bac
and forth to the hospital?" He tickled her bare midriff wit
one bow end and dropped it, placing both hands flat on e
ther side of her face and against the refrigerator.

"Will's not in the hospital. Are you crazy?" The refrig
erator was cold against her bare legs and back.

"Yeah. Crazy about you. Crazy enough to drive all da
to ask you a couple of questions." He leaned right over he
anchoring her to the humming appliance, and nibbled at he
ear. "Nice earrings, angel."

Annie hummed all over.

He was wearing charcoal-gray slacks and a beautiful whi
shirt. He'd even worn a tie, she noticed in her daze, and sl
reached out, holding on to the discreetly patterned gray-or
blue piece of fabric. All dressed up, his hair smoothed bacl
and a gleam in his eyes as he'd pinned her against her r
frigerator door, Ben Jackson looked like her very own sp
cial Christmas present delivered a little bit late.

"If you're here because you think we need help, we don'
We're fine. Nobody's having nightmares, nobody's sick an
my job is very nice, thank you, and that's what I told Gal
when I wrote him, and, oh, Ben, what are you doing?" sl
wailed.

"I'm kissing you, Annie Conroy. At least I'm about to."
He lifted his hand above her head. "I've come for my present. You said anything is possible."

"What?" She looked up to see a bedraggled mistletoe
twig an inch above her head.

"Merry Christmas, Annie," he whispered, and sure
enough, he was kissing her, pinning her between the humming refrigerator and himself, and oh, she'd said anything
was possible, and she'd meant it, meant it, but she'd waited
so long and almost given up hope.

But here he was. And in his intent hazel eyes, she saw
herself reflected, her eyes shining with all the love she had
to give.

"I never thought I could love anyone but I love you, Annie Conroy." He nuzzled her neck and shivers quickened
through her. "You can't even begin to know how much, but
if you'll give me a chance, I'll prove it, every waking minute for the rest of my life. I know I'm a lousy prospect as a
family man, I have no idea how to be a father to Will and
Katie, but I swear to you, no matter what, I'll never walk
away from you. You've got me—if you want me—for better or worse. You and your kids are everything I want out of
life. *Everything*." He kissed her deeper, sending ripples of
need from her toes to the lobes of her ears, and then, his
breath curling into her, he whispered again, "Merry
Christmas, Angel-Annie."

"Oh, Ben," Annie murmured, laughing, "Happy Valentine's Day."

On top of the refrigerator, Katie's hula doll, its battery
jostled on by a sudden thump against the appliance, swished
her plastic grass skirt beguilingly next to a large, heart-shaped valentine.

Annie didn't even see Katie and Will when they peered
around the doorway, didn't hear their giggles.

Wrapping her arms around Ben, running her hands urgently over his smooth cotton shirt, she kissed him back with all the love in her, matching his hunger with her own, the seesaw balanced.

She could wait for explanations.

There would be time.

She knew how this story ended.

*   *   *   *   *

**HE'S MORE THAN
A MAN, HE'S
ONE OF OUR**

**REBEL DAD
Kristin Morgan**

When Linc Rider discovered he was a father, he was determined to find his son and take him back. But he found that Eric already had a home with his adoptive mother, Jillian Fontenot. The choice wouldn't be easy: take the boy from such a beautiful, loving woman or leave his son behind. And soon it was too late to tell Jillian the real reason he'd spent so many days in her home—and in her arms....

Join Linc in his search for family—and love—in Kristin Morgan's REBEL DAD. Available in January—only from Silhouette Romance!

Fall in love with our Fabulous Fathers!

Silhouette
R O M A N C E™

FF194

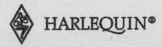

UNDER THE MISTLETOE

*Where's the best place to find love
this holiday season?* UNDER THE MISTLETOE,
*of course! In this special collection, some of
your favorite authors celebrate the joy of the
season and the thrill of romance.*

#976 DADDY'S ANGEL by Annette Broadrick
#977 ANNIE AND THE WISE MEN by Lindsay Longford
#978 THE LITTLEST MATCHMAKER by Carla Cassidy
#979 CHRISTMAS WISHES by Moyra Tarling
#980 A PRECIOUS GIFT by Jayne Addison
#981 ROMANTICS ANONYMOUS by Lauryn Chandler

Available in December from

Silhouette

ROMANCE™

SRXMAS

He staked his claim…

HONOR BOUND

by
New York Times
Bestselling Author

previously published under the pseudonym Erin St. Claire

As Aislinn Andrews opened her mouth to scream, a hard
hand clamped over her face and she found herself face-
to-face with Lucas Greywolf, a lean, lethal-looking
Navajo and escaped convict who swore he wouldn't hurt
her— *if* she helped him.

Look for HONOR BOUND at your favorite
retail outlet this January.

Only from…

where passion lives. SBHB

Share in the joys of finding happiness and exchanging the ultimate gift—love—in full-length classic holiday treasures by two bestselling authors

JOAN HOHL
EMILIE RICHARDS

Available in December at
your favorite retail outlet.

Only from  *Silhouette*® where passion lives.

SILHOUETTE.... Where Passion Lives

Don't miss these Silhouette favorites by some of our most popular authors!
And now, you can receive a discount by ordering two or more titles!

Silhouette Desire®

#05751	THE MAN WITH THE MIDNIGHT EYES BJ James	$2.89	☐
#05763	THE COWBOY Cait London	$2.89	☐
#05774	TENNESSEE WALTZ Jackie Merritt	$2.89	☐
#05779	THE RANCHER AND THE RUNAWAY BRIDE Joan Johnston	$2.89	☐

Silhouette Intimate Moments®

#07417	WOLF AND THE ANGEL Kathleen Creighton	$3.29	☐
#07480	DIAMOND WILLOW Kathleen Eagle	$3.39	☐
#07486	MEMORIES OF LAURA Marilyn Pappano	$3.39	☐
#07493	QUINN EISLEY'S WAR Patricia Gardner Evans	$3.39	☐

Silhouette Shadows®

#27003	STRANGER IN THE MIST Lee Karr	$3.50	☐
#27007	FLASHBACK Terri Herrington	$3.50	☐
#27009	BREAK THE NIGHT Anne Stuart	$3.50	☐
#27012	DARK ENCHANTMENT Jane Toombs	$3.50	☐

Silhouette Special Edition®

#09754	THERE AND NOW Linda Lael Miller	$3.39	☐
#09770	FATHER: UNKNOWN Andrea Edwards	$3.39	☐
#09791	THE CAT THAT LIVED ON PARK AVENUE Tracy Sinclair	$3.39	☐
#09811	HE'S THE RICH BOY Lisa Jackson	$3.39	☐

Silhouette Romance®

#08893	LETTERS FROM HOME Toni Collins	$2.69	☐
#08915	NEW YEAR'S BABY Stella Bagwell	$2.69	☐
#08927	THE PURSUIT OF HAPPINESS Anne Peters	$2.69	☐
#08952	INSTANT FATHER Lucy Gordon	$2.75	☐

	AMOUNT	$ _____
DEDUCT:	10% DISCOUNT FOR 2+ BOOKS	$ _____
	POSTAGE & HANDLING	$ _____
	($1.00 for one book, 50¢ for each additional)	
	APPLICABLE TAXES*	$ _____
	TOTAL PAYABLE	$ _____
	(check or money order—please do not send cash)	

To order, complete this form and send it, along with a check or money order for the total above, payable to Silhouette Books, to: *In the U.S.*: 3010 Walden Avenue, P.O. Box 9077, Buffalo, NY 14269-9077; *In Canada*: P.O. Box 636, Fort Erie, Ontario, L2A 5X3.

Name: _____

Address: _____ City: _____

State/Prov.: _____ Zip/Postal Code: _____

*New York residents remit applicable sales taxes.
Canadian residents remit applicable GST and provincial taxes.

SBACK-OD

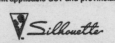